YOSHI OF BETHLEHEM

YOSHI OF BETHLEHEM

By Sharon Mullen

Woodsong Publishing
Seymour, IN

YOSHI OF BETHLEHEM

By Sharon Mullen

First Edition 2018

Woodsong Publishing

5989 Spring Meadow Lane

Seymour, IN 47274

www.woodsongpublishing.com

ISBN 978-0-9979146-8-9

Printed in the USA

Dedicated especially to my husband
and to my father and second mother.

Also dedicated to family, friends,
and a great publisher who supported me in this
writing effort.

And with deep thankfulness to
The Good Shepherd.

Chapter 1: The Fight

Darkness descended quickly over the Judaean Mountains. I had tired from running a great distance and had settled into a slower gait. I was supposed to be the protector for my brother and our sheep. But now they were somewhere being run by a band of Roman thieves. And my brother had been injured by the blow from a soldier! I was wont to believe in the good of people, but as I walked and thought of my flock, I could not help but feel disappointed and disgusted by the blatant disregard of the Roman soldiers for both the lives of me, my brother, and also of my flock. It was humiliating to blow the horn of alarm, knowing Joseph would inform Father of the events of the day…

My thoughts went to Joseph who was no doubt by now at home being nursed by Mother and Sister.

"God," I prayed silently, "let Joseph be okay."

I thought of my flock: of Rema whose leg was strained and mending from having been caught in a hole during the week, and of Lazarus who was old and always had trouble keeping up with the younger sheep. And I thought of the ewes and ram lambs who were possibly being run too fast and too far in a day. And I again thought of my dear Jerusha. Her time to lamb was at hand; a long, hard run could mean death for both her and her unborn.

"Oh, God of Abraham, Isaac, and Jacob, please help me find my flock and rescue it," I said as I began to quicken my pace again.

I was about to enter a treed area which marked the outer edge of our land and began the property of our neighbor. It was in our field before this line of trees that I had said farewell to Amariah. It seemed a lifetime ago that he had been the chief shepherd as I now am. How would he have handled this situation?

I now passed onto the land of our neighbor, Jacob, whose name actually means "supplanter." His property had two particularly scrubby lines of acacia trees on each side of the path, almost as if knowing the heart of the owner. On our land, the same trees grew large and tall. We were not often in communication with this neighbor; he was a Roman sympathizer who was quick to report any infraction of the untenable Roman laws which governed us, especially when it came to taxes. Jacob made it his business to poke about in others' business to report any new animal births or increased grain production so that a Jewish family could be visited by the Romans to collect more taxes.

As I thought of Jacob, I remembered Lydia's future husband. Although I was considerably younger, I remember the talk about when the Romans went to his parents' home to collect tax on an alleged sale of a horse. The gossip was that Jacob had reported this sale. But the chestnut mare was still in their stable when the Romans came. There had been no sale. However, the Romans argued that this mare was the horse that was reported to have been sold. In the exchange of angry words, a sword was drawn, and Lydia's future husband was fatally wounded.

"Oh, God," I prayed, "please deliver us from these Romans!"

As I walked and considered that, unless the Roman thieves were unwise and chose to take a much more narrow and mountainous and thus dangerous route away from Bethlehem, they would have to cross the land of Jacob. Perhaps he was part of this robbery and I would find my sheep grazing on his property.

My mind was too full of thoughts to realize that just ahead of me danger stalked.

"What was that?" I mused.

There had been a sound; I thought it sounded like someone whistling. I wished I had been more intent on studying the path and my surroundings. If a whistle, I might be closer to the Romans than I realized. I needed to find them without being found out myself, and then I would wait for Father to help with retrieval of our flock.

I had no time to further contemplate the sound or my next move. All I could remember is being jumped on from above—he sprang onto me from the branch of a tree. My body slammed to the ground in one huge thump!

"Oh, God..." I screamed, "help me!"

We rolled and tussled on the ground; he was large and strong.

"Must keep my staff in hand..." I thought as my opponent wrapped himself almost entirely around me.

Yoshi of Bethlehem

I knew my staff was inadequate for his size, but I also knew I had to hold onto it, as it was my only defense and also my offensive weapon. I could feel his hot breath on my face, and somehow in the havoc, I had gotten a mouthful of hair.

As we rolled, I saw a large rock to my right. I needed to get to that rock!

I used what little leverage I had with him draped around me to strike his head with my staff. I was enraged and strengthened by that rage; once, twice, three times I slammed the staff's bowed end into his face. More blows; I lost count of the blows, but I could tell his grip was loosening. The blows with my staff seemed effective, yet he still clung to me.

I was striking as much as I could and wrangling us to the right; the rock was closer. It would prove my salvation.

I was reaching for the rock when he took a renewed swipe which hit me across my face. Excruciating pain gripped me, but it also gave me seconds to jump from his clutches and grab the rock.

I put my whole weight into a pounding to his head. He was up from the ground now, too. He was huge, and his eyes were glazed with anger and hatred.

I had to deliver another hard hit. His getting up afforded the few seconds I needed to regain my equilibrium. I reared back and fell into him as hard as my young body would go.

"Lord, God, I need you!"

I got this blow right between his eyes. He was dazed. And it was the opportunity to strike the final blow.

The mountain lion lay in a heap.

I was not happy that I had to kill him, but I was delighted that it was he, not me, who died.

I cried to the Lord, "Thank you for your protection and for strengthening me!"

I used my inner tunic to wipe my face. I assessed that it was not as torn as I expected from the pain. I also gave God praise for that. Even though my face was lacerated from the lash of his paw, and my sides were pierced from his claws digging through my robe into my skin, I was upright and alive. It could have been worse for me.

My water-skin had been flattened in the scuffle. My clothes were wet but with water and thankfully not my own blood. But no water meant I had nothing to drink as I now thirsted, and I had no water to cleanse my wounds.

Yoshi of Bethlehem

I sat for a short time to regain my strength. I was shaking from the fight, but I felt a sense of pride for having come through it without being greatly harmed. I looked at the crumpled beast, and my body gave an involuntary shudder. I was eager to move on. The flock was still in danger.

As I got up, I realized I was much more fatigued from the fight than I thought. I would need to move along the path a bit more slowly, and certainly with more caution. But that would not matter, I would get to my flock even if it were the middle of the night. I set off again.

I did not realize it at the time, but the fight provided valuable time for my father who was now moving along the path in my direction. He had heard the horn of alarm and had gone to his brother-in-law's house and borrowed his donkey to get to our camp. The donkey was a blessing for his journey toward the sheep. He knew he needed a bit more speed than his legs would provide.

I had only covered a short distance when I felt the need to stop and sit again. The mountain lion now lay behind me on the road, but the battle with him had effectively taken much of my strength. I went to sit, but instead, I collapsed on the path beneath the overhanging of a tree.

Sharon Mullen

My thoughts wandered to where this all began, how I got here, and I questioned how it would end. Perhaps I should back up and share some details of my story and introduce you to my family.

Chapter 2: Bethlehem

I live in Israel, a diminutive, yet historically and spiritually powerful country! Some would like to think of my country as insignificant, but they cannot. God has been, is, and always will be Ruler of Israel. He will bless those that bless Israel.

And within the small country of Israel is the tiny city where I was born, Bethlehem.

Let me make my introduction; I am Yoshi of Bethlehem, a shepherd and second son of Miriam and Joel, born of the lineage of Aaron. We are a family of humble means, currently both offering administrative service to Temple (through my Uncle Roshan's generosity, which I will discuss) and tending sheep. My mother, Miriam, is loving and of kind spirit, but she is of poor health. My father, Joel, is a generous man and is as industrious as he is tender-hearted. Some see this latter attribute as weakness, but not me. It is he who tended our flock before me and instilled into me great respect for these animals. It is he who raises beautiful goats for milk and cheese-making and raises fowl for eggs and meat. He also grows delicious figs and pomegranates in the temperamental Bethlehem soil. It is my father to whom many of the poor in our area turn for help.

My sister, Lydia, is second oldest. She has been tasked with running the household due to my mother's delicate health. She was once betrothed; gifts were exchanged between families and a marriage contract sealed, but as I already mentioned, her husband died from injuries he received from Roman soldiers who had come to collect taxes from him. I do not know that whole story; my family, especially Lydia, will not speak of it as it makes her sad. After the death of her husband, the village blacksmith, whose wife had died—leaving him with eight young children—came asking my father for Lydia in marriage. My father refused his offer. I heard Lydia once say that she was relieved not to marry him.

My younger brother is Joseph, who is a bright mischief-making lad. Joseph ultimately becomes my shepherding student, and he is worthy of the staff!

Yoshi of Bethlehem

Until their deaths three years ago, my grandparents lived in our household. Ruth, my grandmother, was plump and jovial. Her cheeks seemed to always suggest pomegranates to me. She could make everyone around her happy they were living, even if they were in poor circumstances. My grandfather, Amos, was wise in Scripture. He tended our flock before my father, but his chief role was in ministry. He was often called upon to judge disputes, to marry, and to call to people's remembrance God's greatness through the feasts and festivals we Jews celebrate. Grandfather vehemently disliked the Romans living in and controlling our land. The Promised Land, Israel, was dear to him, and he found the presence of these pagan Gentiles very sobering. And my grandfather, since the first time I have any memory of him, always made it known that Messiah was coming. How he dreamed and prayed for that day! Grandfather felt the Romans were ushering in the era when Messiah would come and save us from their oppression. Grandfather knew that the Prophet Micah had foretold that Messiah would come from Bethlehem:

> But thou, Bethlehem, though thou be smallest
> among the thousands in Judah, yet out of thee shall
> He come forth...

Sharon Mullen

My grandfather believed for Messiah's appearance and deliverance until his last breath. And not more than one full moon later, grandmother followed him into Sheol. She could not face the future without her Amos.

Mattityahu, or as we call him, Amariah, is my older brother. It is at his prodding that I write the following narrative of my life. Amariah became a Rabbi, a biblical Scholar, a Teacher of The Law. Amariah was once a shepherd in the fields with me. How I idolized him and hoped to be just like him! He tended with great care and with skill. But the winds of change blew onto those fields. How could I know that life would change so drastically so quickly? Amariah was gifted the opportunity to move to Jerusalem with Mother's brother to study The Law. It was an incalculable blessing on many levels.

Although of the line of Aaron, I was born in Bethlehem where my family, many generations previous, had been relocated. Initially, my ancestors were forcefully moved from Jerusalem to Babylon during the reign of Nebuchadnezzar. Some seventy years later, when the walls were being rebuilt during the reign of Cyrus, and families were being urged to return, my family did return to Jerusalem, to Israel, to our Promised Land.

Yoshi of Bethlehem

My ancestors were present when the rebuilt Temple was dedicated. There are many family stories of the joyous return to Jerusalem and of that most glorious event, the dedication of the second Temple. My family's oral history also speaks of it as a bittersweet time since the second Temple was nowhere near the scale in size or grandeur of appurtenances as the first.

As tribal heads returned from Babylon, my returning ancestors were asked to move to Bethlehem to serve in ministry there. That meant leaving Jerusalem and the only home our family had known for many generations (until the exile). And it meant much sacrifice—physically, emotionally and financially—to make that move.

My family's move to Bethlehem at the request of the Priests occurred during a time when rains had not come to Israel for several years. Bethlehem was barren both physically and spiritually. Not only did my ancestors have to contend with re-building their own lives in this new, harsh environment (they had lived in relative comfort both in Jerusalem and in Babylon), they also served others through the ministry. This greatly increased their load. Bethlehem, in its state of decay, meant added burden as my family worked with others who,

13

like themselves, were unaccustomed to the manual labor and the brutal heat they endured as they cleared their land and constructed homes where others' ancestral homes had stood but now lay in ruins. They were not used to the predatory animals they faced daily and at night; they were unaccustomed to the food that grew in this parched Israeli soil; they were strangers to those around them, who, like themselves, had been asked to relocate from Jerusalem. They were unaccustomed to the idea of worship without a grand Temple. But the thing that they were accustomed to, the thing that helped my family through every new and often fierce trial, was their trust in God and in His provision of their territory. Israel was their rightful heritage, and they were dedicated to repatriation to the Promised Land.

By God's grace, our current family land in Bethlehem had become available through the death of a patriarch from another family in Babylon who desired to remain in Babylon. Since this family chose not to return to Bethlehem, they were willing to sell the land to my family. They would not return within a year to redeem that land, as The Law allotted for them. Thus, they permanently transferred ownership.

Yoshi of Bethlehem

My ancestors had been thrifty with the meager earnings they acquired through the years. The purchase of the land in Bethlehem, which we now claim as our heritage, left little funds, but with that paltry sum, they built a home on this newly purchased land. And they continued steadfastly in their knowledge that God would not fail them.

So, what does a Levite who needs work do for a living? My ancestors turned to the occupation of the great King David—shepherding. They purchased several sheep and raised a flock which provided for sacrificial offerings and for animals to sell. In fact, those few sheep bought many generations ago, are the ancestors of my current flock—eighty-eight blessings from God! Not enough sheep to earn great wealth but enough to provide adequately for the family's needs.

Bethlehem, although a small, poor area, has been the source of many great Jewish historical figures:

Rachel was buried here. She had died on the journey that God had asked Israel, her husband (originally known as Jacob), to take with his family. Travel was not easy, and Rachel was with child. She passed from this life to Sheol as she birthed a son, Benjamin. Israel greatly loved Rachel; he had worked for her father, Laban, many years to pay her dowry. But as prophesied, through Israel and Rachel, a great nation rose up. A nation in which I am proud to live and shepherd—Israel.

Ruth and her husband left Bethlehem during a famine. But she records that she went out empty and came back full due to the abundant blessings of God.

David, my greatest hero and Israel's second king, was born and tended sheep here! I cannot say enough wonderful things about brave David. As a lad tending his sheep, he fought a lion and a bear. This, in turn, helped him defeat the largest enemy of all time, Goliath. How proud all of Israel is to name David as a predecessor! And I am pleased to be a shepherd as was King David!

David loved Bethlehem; one time he desired water from a well here during a battle.

From this small, insignificant city, it is foretold that the Messiah would be born. I await the fulfillment of this prophesy, as does all of Israel.

A trip to Jerusalem with my family, when I was still a young lad, heightened my desire to know the Lord more. And He did not disappoint me when I asked to know Him in a more significant way. My writing is an effort to give an account of

Yoshi of Bethlehem

the miraculous happenings in the otherwise mundane life of a
shepherd. Events that shaped the future of the world! And
my effort is put forth in hopes that someone else may come
to know Him.

Chapter 3: Brothers

Amariah has five years more of living than I; Lydia, our beautiful sister, was born between us. Those five years also repre-
sent the number of years Amariah has been gone. Five years
ago we were contented boys both tending the family flock.
Me, by day, and Amariah, by night. We had many hours together to play, to plan, and to pray when the sheep's stom-
achs were full and the high sun caused them to seek rest and
shade.

Our father taught us to pray so that everything else we
did might be blessed. We began the day and ended our time
together with prayer.

When time in the fields permitted, Amariah and I crafted
our fun. We had a favorite game. It was the "Saul and David"
game and involved hiding from one another: among the sheep,
in caves, or among the trees and tall grasses in the fields.

One of us would be Saul, and the other would be David; David would hide, and Saul would be tasked with finding him. Of course, both of us wanted to be David! It was a high honor to play David.

One particular day when I was seven years old and Amariah was twelve, while the sheep were ruminating and relaxing, we decided to play "Saul and David." I was Saul; as David, Amariah was given time to hide. He found a hole in the ground large enough to slip into and far away enough to avoid my hearing his movements. This hole was actually in our main pasture but heretofore had gone unnoticed among some large rocks.

I spent quite some time searching for "David," as the sun began to drop from being overhead in the sky and the sheep were interested in grazing once again. Amariah, or, David, could not be found. Then suddenly he let out a shout louder than a shofar!

"Eeeeyaa," Amariah screamed. "Brother help me!"

I looked in his direction to see him partially stooped and pulling at his leg.

"Come quickly!"

Yoshi of Bethlehem

"I am coming," I shouted. I avoided a flock stampede by maneuvering carefully past them in high spirit but not running, which could scare them into a panic.

I reached Amariah to see him working at freeing his sandal from a rock that had shifted. But he was also jabbing his staff into a hole. I thought that very odd.

"Yoshi, get my foot free."

I could shift the heavy rock easily, as I was above it. But Amariah continued prodding his staff into the hole from which he had evidently secreted himself. With the rock shifted off his foot and two feet with which to work, Amariah was more intent on his fight with his staff in the hole. But what was he fighting?

"What is it, Amariah?" I questioned.

"It's a snake … I think a saw-scaled viper."

As I was delayed in finding his good hiding spot, Amariah had dozed off. He woke to a familiar sound and instinctively knew it was an ill-tempered snake rubbing the sides of its body together making a rasping sound! He had fallen asleep in the lair of a poisonous serpent. He immediately tried to jump out of the hole but had gotten his sandal caught. He grabbed his staff and began to fight the snake while trying to wrest his foot from the rock. And the snake was intent upon living!

Again and again, Amariah hit the snake, but it kept striking at him. At one point, once his foot was released, the snake was actually on the top of Amariah's staff. It looked like Moses in the wilderness with the bronze serpent atop a pole. But it dropped back into the hole.

Realizing that Amariah was becoming exhausted from the heat of the day and the determination of the snake to live, I took my staff and began to assist in the battle.

Somewhere in the course of this mayhem, the snake was pitched by Amariah. However, it landed on my neck. This was totally unsettling! I ran like a jackal, crying and screaming louder than Amariah, but in my hysteria I was unable to remove the snake from around my neck! I was so afraid that I didn't even consider my screams might stampede the sheep.

Thankfully, Amariah knew he had finally pierced the snake through and ran to me to tell me to stop while he removed the thing – now dead – with his staff. As a shorter combatant, but an unwitting target, I realized how utterly discomfiting it is to have a dead viper around one's neck.

Yoshi of Bethlehem

I gladly gave Amariah the "win" for our game of "Saul and David." My brave brother never told anyone of my fear that day. Instead, he talked of the event at times to reassure me that God is always with me to help in times of trouble and in times of fear! Our prayer that night was for fear not to be our companion.

Amariah prayed, "God, who created all things, thank you for your love. And we thank you also tonight that we do not live in fear. You are always with us, protecting and watching over us in the same way Yoshi and I guard our flock. We thank you for the gift of safety and the gift of a good day. The Lord bless you and keep you; The Lord make His face shine upon you, and be gracious to you; The Lord lift up His countenance upon you, and give you peace."

As I drifted off to sleep, and Amariah went to guard the flock overnight, my thought was, "Amariah is a wonderful brother."

But our time together in the Bethlehem fields tending sheep, worshiping our Maker, and enjoying each other's company ended at Amariah's thirteenth year. Our Uncle Roshan had come from Jerusalem. He would return home with Amariah. The plans had been made between Uncle and Father.

Amariah would begin formal studies and assume Levitical teaching and Temple duties in Jerusalem. For Uncle Roshan, this was the opportunity for doing his part for the family to once again be represented at Temple in Jerusalem. It was a high honor.

Uncle Roshan's wife had died and left no children; Amariah would become the son he never had. He would take on all financial obligation for Amariah. For Amariah, this was a first-born male child's dream: to be able to have formal study in Jerusalem and to be instructed and take part in priestly duties at Temple.

Uncle Roshan did not wish to tarry in Bethlehem. The arrangements between adults were sealed; all that was needed was Amariah.

I shall always remember that day. It was unusually cool, and the sheep seemed of great appetite. Amariah and I had walked them to a new area to graze, the farthest point of our land's line which connected to our neighbor, Jacob. It was early afternoon. Amariah had dozed for a time, and we were settled in for the sheep to graze and had decided to build a small fire which Amariah would keep burning through the night

Yoshi of Bethlehem

watch. And if we were fortunate, we would later find a bird in our wooden trap to grill on this fire for our dinner.

I am not sure which of us saw her first, but we both saw the outline of a young girl walking briskly in our direction. We knew this to be Lydia from her walk and from the desert rose colored headdress she typically wore. In the field, no one ever came merely to visit; anyone walking this distance had a message to deliver. Such a message!

We called to her in unison, "Sister!"

She was still far enough away not to respond. Once she reached us, she was out of breath and signaled to let her rest for a moment. From the pocket of her robe, she dropped scant provisions as she sat panting.

"Why so few provisions?" I wondered, as we gobbled down the freshly baked food.

After she caught her breath, she delivered the message about Uncle Roshan's arrival and arrangements for Amariah to return with him to Jerusalem. Lydia informed me that Father requested that I nap when possible and plan the night watches, along with the day watches, because Amariah was leaving and would not be returning. Uncle Roshan was intent upon immediate departure for Jerusalem.

And so, with a hasty hug and a promise that one day we would meet again, he was gone. Amariah: my mentor, my protector, my friend and playmate, my brother; Amariah would never be back to these fields.

I watched him and Sister quickly walk away. Even after our many discussions of God being with us and having no fear, I cried large drops of fear-filled tears. Thankfully, Amariah did not turn around as he walked away; I preferred that he not see my tears.

Chapter 4: Jerusha

After Amariah left, Father came to the fields to provide relief to me at various times through the years; when he was there, he always took the night watch. That meant I could get rest without needing to be half awake!

It was during one of these visits that Father came especially to inform me that he and Mother had spoken to Jehoram and Topetha of Bethlehem concerning their daughter, Asara, who was of the age of contract to marry. An agreement had been reached for her to become my bride at her sixteenth year, which was yet five years away. All that was needed was my consent, which I provided. Father would take this consent back and make the matter known to the community in Bethlehem. He informed me that I would thus be gifted the ram and lamb of my choice, and any offspring they produced during this time of my shepherding would go towards

27

my livelihood. This was my ketubah, an agreement outlining the responsibility of each partner.

I had hopes of marrying, but I did not know if or when a maid would be chosen. In putting together my thoughts and recollections of this girl, I remember both of us being very young and Asara playing with her sisters who all came to play with Lydia. We young boys always played our own games, so we have never spoken to one another, but I do remember her as a very young girl running and giggling with Lydia and the other sisters. Her family, too, was part of the diaspora and then the return from exile. As well, they were not originally from Bethlehem but from Shechem and of the Tribe of Manasseh. Her father was a craftsman working with beautiful wood. Particularly, he built furnishings for houses. Some were too fine and too costly for local use, those he would take to Jerusalem to sell.

For the marriage ketubah, I chose a new lamb named Jerusha, and a ram lamb Joseph had named Adam. They were both healthy and handsome sheep. They should produce beautiful offspring which would be used as gifts offered to Asara's family as well as to start our flock.

This was an exciting expectation ... marriage.

Yoshi of Bethlehem

But for now, my mind and work were on the flock, since most of the time I tended them day and night. I knew it would be several years before a marriage ceremony would take place.

At four months from Amariah's departure, my younger brother joined me in the fields. Father said I was a man and could care for and tutor Joseph. Joseph reminded me of myself when I came to the fields to assist Amariah. I had been about the same age, as eager to learn and as full of energy as Joseph.

His coming did not prove an immediate relief to my oversight of the flock, since Joseph was unaccustomed to their care. But I taught Joseph, as Amariah had taught me, to care for our sheep, as my father had taught Amariah. I reflected on David and his many years between being anointed as King of Israel and having to flee from King Saul who was jealous of him and wanted him dead. When David's family members— who were being threatened by Saul—and a ragtag army of discontents gathered at the Cave of Adullam, he had to guide the men into becoming a good army. Many were unskilled in warfare; most were not equipped to fight. But God used those men in a mighty way to bring David to the promise

of being king. So, too, was my Joseph coming to the fields
to shepherd; he was neither skilled nor equipped, but God
helped me as I guided him, just as God had helped David train
his army.

Joseph did prove a quick learner, a patient animal over-
seer, and great support to have in the fields. The four months
after Amariah first left, and I was mostly alone, had been arduous; I had to nap when possible to keep both the day and
night watches. Often, I quoted David's words when fatigue,
fear, or loneliness came over me,

"The Lord is my Shepherd, I shall not want. He maketh
me to lie down in green pastures: he leadeth me beside the
still waters. He restoreth my soul: he leadeth me in the paths
of righteousness for his name's sake. Yea, though I walk
through the valley of the shadow of death, I will fear no evil:
for thou art with me; thy rod and thy staff they comfort me.
Thou preparest a table before me in the presence of mine enemies: thou anointest my head with oil; my cup runneth over.
Surely goodness and mercy shall follow me all the days of my
life: and I will dwell in the house of the Lord forever."

I thought of Amariah on many occasions while shepherding. At times travelers would bring us notice of Amariah from

Yoshi of Bethlehem

Uncle Roshan. He was one of the best scholars of his class and was also being used for Temple service. I was very happy for Amariah but also still sad he left, since I could not be certain we would ever meet again.

Time in the fields moves quickly. Now, some five years since his joining me, Joseph and I have fallen into a routine which provides support for each of us as we care for our flock at all times.

Although timid and easily frightened, our sheep were remarkably smart, or at least I thought this. Take Jerusha for example, my favorite ewe, who was also part of my marriage gift. She was nearing the age of the passing of five Passovers. Other ewe's young were chosen for the Passover sacrifice, but her offspring had never been chosen. They were never entirely without blemish, but they were lively, healthy animals—and considered to be "mine," thus, they were the progeny for the formation of my own flock!

Jerusha was with lamb and nearing term. The days seemed especially humid, and no wind blew to relieve the hot air that hung over the flock. At least the nights were cool. I often wondered if David, as a shepherd, suffered from the heat and cold, or whether he grew accustomed to it as I have.

31

Jerusha had to be especially careful of her steps; she could not afford to stumble and cast her unborn. And I had the extra pressure of making sure none of the others were frightened enough to run. One frightened sheep could create a situation where all the sheep will run erratically and far, just because one of the flock takes off. And a ewe about to lamb would almost assuredly lose her offspring in a high-spirited run!

It was Sabbath. We had moved the flock to an area of pasture that offered fresh fodder and had a well that father had dug many years before. Being in this area for Sabbath was nice. Besides the green field and abundant water, this was our established "home pen," so named because it was closest to our actual home in Bethlehem. One side of the enclosure was made from an outcrop of rocks; the other sides were created with brush and sticks or small saplings which had been gathered and planted through the years and made a thick hedge. Save for repairing a few obvious areas on the brush sides, Joseph and I could settle in to use this pasture for several days before moving again.

Yes, it felt great to have this Sabbath spent closer to our home and in an area of relative ease. The flock, too, seemed at rest after the move yesterday to this pasture. Joseph and I would spend the day in prayer and worship and rest.

It was mid-afternoon, and we drowsed in the heat of the day. I had finished mid-day minchah, which seemed the most challenging time of prayer. I was at guard and leaning on the gate to the pen while Joseph was some distance away resting by the well.

As I sat there in a state of half sleep, from beyond the outcrop of rocks, I heard the sound of a flute or wind instrument of some nature. But the music ceased almost as quickly as it came.

"Was I dreaming?" I thought. I glanced at the flock who were resting and ruminating. I saw Jerusha sleeping contentedly. The sheer lull of activity of the herd made me yearn for a rest. I closed my eyes for a short time of sleep; however, I dare not fall into deep sleep at my post even on the Sabbath.

But wait! Was that the sound from that instrument again?

Again, the sound was light and quickly made, but it sounded closer. I glanced over at Joseph, but he did not seem to notice; for he did not stir. The flock did not notice; they had not stirred.

I was beginning to feel some unease. I feigned sleep but truly was listening intently for any other sounds that did not belong to the flock or Joseph.

As I sat motionlessly, the instrument sounded again—louder—which meant closer, and it was at a very short interval. My thoughts raced as I was unsure of the portend of this sound.

"What should I do?" I pondered.

It did not take long for the answer to the instrument's sounding to make sense. With great fierceness and loud shouts, a group of men jumped down from the rock wall into the pen. Roman soldiers! I had seen their attire before. They wielded clubs and ran screaming through the sheep attempting to move them to the gate.

It was apparent they were intent on stealing the flock. My father had told stories of their penchant for thievery! An important question whirled in my mind: "Would they run the sheep or try to walk them away?"

Joseph was closest to the rock wall and one soldier rapped him with his club across his head just as he was rising. He fell, motionless. I took up my staff to fight, but the sheep, having been frightened by the Romans' screams, knocked me to the ground. The sheep were now pushing against the gate next to me.

"Whoa now, calm, calm, whoosh, whoosh," I tried to quiet the flock. "Whoosh, whoosh..." I continued in my calmest voice.

Two of the Romans were now on me, and I had lost my staff when knocked down by the sheep. I had no weapon.

"Help me, God...Yea though I walk through..."

The pen gate could no longer handle the press of the sheep, and it parted. The sheep, now alarmed, began to run. This was a terrible sight, but it saved me from the Romans' clubs.

One of the two Romans pushed me down under the hooves of my flock. All I could do was roll and try to escape. Several sheep stepped on me as I struggled to get out of their way.

The Romans continued to yell and follow the sheep out of the pen. When I regained my composure, I could see five soldiers trailing the sheep. They seemed to be working to quiet them and keep them together. It was no small task since they were now panicked.

I turned to Joseph, since he was my biggest concern at the moment. He was trying to sit up, and blood flowed from his temple. I ran to him.

"Joseph, Joseph, my brother, are you badly hurt?" I asked.

"No, Yoshi, I don't know...but my head aches. I am able to see and to talk. What do we do?" he asked, as he applied his tunic to his temple to staunch the flow of blood.

"You remain here," I ordered. "They will not return. I will blow the ram's horn signaling danger and the need for assistance. When Father comes, send him to me. I will follow the sheep."

I grabbed the unharmed horn which we always keep with us and sounded the alarm: one long blow; silence; another long blow; silence; a third long blow and silence. Our family's alarm, signaling an emergency.

"Yoshi, I wish you would not go alone. Wait until Father comes. Or at least let me go too." And with that last comment, Joseph attempted to stand but slumped to his knees.

"Joseph, listen to me, you must stay. I must leave right away. It will be harder to find them the farther they run as darkness falls."

Yoshi of Bethlehem

"God be with you, Yoshi. Take the horn, in case you need it again."

I turned to find my staff some distance from where I had been resting at the pen gate. As I reached for the staff, I realized that I, too, was somewhat dizzy from the unkind push of the Romans under the hooves of some of the flock. It seemed my right arm, my stronger arm, had a dull ache. But I was thankful neither Joseph nor I had been killed. It appeared that the sheep were the only objects of these Romans' interest.

With staff in hand, I headed down the main path the flock had taken. The sheep were actually moving along the path in the direction from which we had recently moved. But, of course, I could not know how far my flock would run.

The area to which I was following the sheep and Romans was hillier than the home pen from which these sheep had just been freed. I had run a considerable distance; my head was pounding either from the sun, or from the sheep's hooves, or the soldier's strong shove. But I knew I could not delay moving forward, as the lives of my sheep depended on me.

As I pushed on, I wondered if my hero, David, ever had his flock stolen. Indeed, there were no Romans in his day, but there were Philistines and other groups who at times plundered and pillaged the Israelites' camps and cities.

As my thirst and fatigue became evident, my steps became more difficult. But eighty-eight sheep were counting on me to save them. My family and our financial survival depended on the sheep. And I realized, too, my marriage to Asara was predicated on a gift from these sheep!

I made my way, continuing to follow the recent treading of the brush by the flock. It seemed that the width of the herd was diminishing. This meant their frenzy was lessening. Also, the path itself was narrowing, which would keep them from running as wildly and swiftly.

My thoughts turned to my dear Jerusha who was close to lambing. A run could be fatal.

"Oh, God of Abraham, Isaac, and Jacob, please protect my flock!" I cried out to the Lord in the heavens. In praying that prayer, I had no idea the danger that was about to confront me. But in retrospect, I now realize God heard and answered my prayer. And He would protect my flock.

Chapter 5: Father

That is the backstory that brought me to this place. I lay for a time on the path beneath the shade of an overhanging tree, not really wanting to sleep but knowing I was physically spent. As I lay there, I must have drifted off to sleep, for the next sound I heard was hooves. And I had no time to respond to them by moving from their path.

I looked up from my prone position, in great relief.

"Father!" I cried.

"Yoshi, my son," said Father. "Are you hurt?"

As if with one fluid motion, Father dismounted the donkey, covered the few paces to where I lay, and wiped my face with his sleeve.

"What has happened to your face?" asked Father.

"Father, did you not see it on the way? I killed a mountain lion!"

"But there was no mountain lion on the road as I came."

"Oh, Father, yes, it is but a short distance from here. I had to stop here for a rest before continuing. It took all my strength to free myself from him and to kill him!"

Father gave me a quizzical look and lifted a water skin from his belt, passed it to me, and I took a long drink.

"You mount, and I will walk, Yoshi."

I would have normally refused such an offer, but my ebbing strength made me glad that Uncle's donkey was now part of our rescue entourage. What a precious blessing to have the donkey with us. He was an unusually marked beast. His forehead looked as if God had painted a large picture of the sun on his fur. The beast had made Father's getting to me all the faster, and it would help us as we moved on to rescue our sheep.

"How curious that the lion is gone," said Father.

That was odd to me as well. Father would have had to pass him on this path. But we had no time nor interest in walking back to investigate my fighting grounds.

The shadows were beginning to lengthen, signaling day's end. Father and I quietly discussed what had happened that day as we walked and rode the beast further into the land of

Yoshi of Bethlehem

Jacob. We knew that we could not go much further before nightfall.

We came upon a grove of sycamore trees and decided to make this our evening camp. Father tied the donkey to a tree. We discussed whether to make a fire. It can be very cool at night in Bethlehem, and a fire is a welcomed friend, but we also knew the Romans, now walking a flock, could not be too far ahead. No doubt they would be watching behind them for any evidence of being followed. The decision was made to forgo the fire. I was exhausted, so this decision—which meant no gathering of wood—was quite acceptable to me.

Father had brought bread and cheese and water which we ate and drank for dinner. I realized how hungry I was when he produced the round, small, hard loaves of both bread and cheese from the inside pouch of his tunic. I wished I could eat all he brought, but I realized we would need this to last. Father saw my hunger and acted as if he were not that hungry and gave me half of his ration for that night.

"I will say our prayer for this night, Yoshi," Father said, when I finished eating.

"Hear o Israel, the Lord our God is One. Lord be our God as we walk in your ways, and keep your commandments

41

and as we hearken unto your voice. You have saved us this day with your mighty arm and with your great power. The Lord be blessed..."

I do not believe I heard much of his continued prayer. Sleep came to me without delay. But one thought occurred to me as I closed my eyes. I felt safe; my father was here. Just the presence of Father brought newfound peace.

It was still dark, with only light from twinkling stars over-head, when Father nudged me awake. As I moved to get up, I realized what a toll had been exacted on my muscles by the fight with the mountain lion! And the crusty dried-blood on my face bore the evidence of the beast's paw. But the thought of our flock made me sit up to ready myself to go.

Father whispered the day's plans. We would break later to eat. And we would need to move ahead more cautiously. It appeared that the Romans had taken the flock not as sport, to run them and leave them in a panic. If that had been the case, we would have already found parts of the flock along the path. But these soldiers had taken them and walked them in an orderly fashion, keeping them together. They were probably interested in selling them. So, we could be in close proximity to them, as I had not lost much time in following them yesterday after setting off in a run.

Yes, we would need to move now more quietly. That made Father and me think of uncle's donkey. He could be quite obstinate and then quite noisy when being obstinate! Father looked toward the donkey…then he looked a second time. I then looked at the donkey.

"Where is the donkey, Father?" I asked.

We both bolted up and over to the tree where he had been tied the night before. He was gone. Father and I tiptoed about the trees in search of the beast. He was not there.

So, we were faced with our second mystery. The first, what happened to the mountain lion? The second, what happened to Uncle's donkey?

"Do you think the mountain lion is alive and could have taken him, Father?" I asked.

"No. Someone has untied and taken him," he whispered, "and may God mete out His judgment on the one who has taken the jack. I pray that we find him to return him to my brother-in-law."

And with these mysteries unsolved, we loaded the pouches of our robes with the few items we had and set out walking. On this day, I was glad to have my staff providing a bit of support.

Father walked in front and kept a watch on the dark vista. It would be hard to see a person—or animal—moving in the dark in which we now walked. And we were unfamiliar with Jacob's terrain.

We had covered quite a distance, still enveloped by the dark and in a grove of olive trees, when Father stumbled over something. As he regained his poise, I caught up to him.

He had stumbled over a newborn lamb, still in the water sack with the umbilical cord attached. There was no doubt; this was Jerusha's lamb. She was the only ewe so ready to lamb. My stomach churned. Where was my Jerusha then?

It did not take long for us to scan the area and see her still body. Father bent over her. She was dead.

"Yoshi," Father said quietly, "she is gone. It is apparent that she had been attacked by a large animal, the marks on her body prove that. We can gather a few limbs here quickly and quietly to cover her," Father offered.

Yoshi of Bethlehem

Father placed the tree limbs over her, leaving her face uncovered. It had not been scarred by the animal's paws, which was not typical when being savaged. I looked at her face in the scant light from the heavens. She looked beautiful. I would miss my favorite ewe. She was a daughter of the first lamb that I saw born when I came to shepherd with Amariah. And, of most importance, she was the mother of the offspring for my ketubah.

We walked on. I was now glad that it was still dark enough that my father could not see me clearly. The sadness of this loss made water run from my eyes and down my cheeks. I wanted to be a man, but this was a significant loss.

Chapter 6: Rescue

The sky was beginning to lighten when we heard an awful scream. It came from the path directly ahead. We quickly but quietly followed the trail as it wound up a small hill. We stopped and looked down into a valley. From our vantage point behind a boulder, we could see the Romans camped a short distance below in a circle of stones. And there, too, was our flock!

But what about that scream? There it was again, along with sounds of loud shouting. And it was clear now from whence the cry emanated. A mountain lion— my enemy from the looks of the blood on his head—was attacking one of the soldiers. The mountain lion had him by the arm and upper body and was tossing him from side to side. The soldiers, with their short swords brandished, were attempting to strike the lion but apparently did not know how to do so with their comrade being tossed so wildly.

Finally, one of the soldiers moved behind the big cat. The soldier struck him on the back with the sword. The mountain lion immediately dropped the first soldier and with a powerful turn and swipe of his sizable front paw had laid the second soldier to the ground.

I wanted to shout out, but I held my words. Father motioned for us to be very quiet and stay behind the bolder to see how this would play out. The sheep were being spooked. They were confined in the area by a circle of stones, but they had both paths that lead in and out of the rocky area as egresses.

The soldiers were finally gaining control of the mountain lion. Again and again, the three soldiers, still on their feet and not wounded by the lion, struck him. The mountain lion shrieked in pain and continued to strike out at the soldiers. He was able to get one last swipe of his paw across the chest of an un-uniformed soldier. The soldier fell back in response. But the other two soldiers felled the final blows across the head of the mountain lion. He dropped limply to the ground.

As if by Divine intervention, about the time the soldiers were finishing the animal kill, the flock began to run. And to run in our direction—toward their home!

Yoshi of Bethlehem

"Thank you, God!" I said aloud with my father motioning for quiet. His preference was that the Romans not know we were present.

We moved to let the stampeding flock get by us. On and on they came. Rema, whose leg had been strained, was being shoved forward by the others. Lazarus was also trotting along as the others frantically ran, but at a slower stride. I thought of my Jerusha. This would not have gone well for her if she were still alive and instinctively running with the flock. Perhaps her death at the hands of a mountain lion was quicker and less painful. I could not know, but I knew I would always feel her loss.

Meanwhile, the two unscathed soldiers below were tending to their fellow soldiers. One of them went out of our sight in the rocky area and returned—with uncle's donkey!

All our mysteries were now solved!

We watched between our flock running past us wildly and the soldiers as they mounted the most wounded soldier and made their way to the path out of this area into Jacob's land. What they did not realize, however, was that the best aid they could hope to acquire was in Bethlehem, which was closer on the path back through our land. They were on a fool's errand to get back to receive help by crossing the land of Jacob, although as a Roman sympathizer, he would no doubt offer them some assistance. And perhaps they were well aware of that.

Father and I quickly followed the sheep. They were now some distance separated from us as they ran wildly, bleating and pushing and shoving one another through smaller path openings.

The day was far from over as we once again shepherded and calmed and led the sheep back to the pen closest to our house. I was glad that Joseph and I had decided that this pen would serve us well for a time and had already moved the flock here before the course of these events.

My father and other men from the area were going to make watches among the shepherds' fields for a time. However, Father and the other men doubted these Romans were physically capable of returning any time soon.

Joseph's head blow had proved very superficial. He would return to the fields right away.

I could rest; my father was in control. Truly, The Father was in control.

Chapter 7: Jerusalem

Zachariah, the High Priest, has gone into Temple to offer
incense. The Temple is magnificent!

I think back, just two days ago, as we neared Jerusalem,
the path widened. There were many travelers. We rounded
the area called "Mount of Olives" due to the large number
of growers of olives. At one point in history, the groves
of olives here were impressive; however, the olive trees are
not as ubiquitous now as then. From here, the path was
high enough to see across the Kidron Valley. There was
Jerusalem. Jerusalem, "the joy of the whole earth." David,
my hero, had used this phrase, and I was now looking upon
Jerusalem which is also known as the City of David. This
was an awesome moment for me. I was seeing the city where
my hero had lived, loved, died. The city he helped build and
make great. The Temple was evident in the distance as its

glistening walls and dome shone in the brilliant sunlight. It was situated atop a white foundational platform, so this also made the splendor of the Temple even more astounding. If this was just a shadow of the former Temple, I wondered how it could have been any lovelier than the Temple I was viewing now from afar. I knew from conversation with Father, however, that the Roman King Herod had made some enhancements to this Temple in an effort to please the Jews.

There were walls around the city; it was apparent some were not in perfect condition, but they made the city itself seem even grander. Several taller buildings were seen; Uncle Roshan had told Father that the Romans had built citadels and palaces for Herod. These might be some of those edifices; I could not be sure. I just wanted to stand and gaze at Jerusalem for hours, maybe days. But Mother's cough interrupted my thoughts. It was time to get her to Uncle Roshan's so she could rest.

I return to the present with my thoughts and to the amazing experience of being on Temple property while the High Priest is offering incense to God. I am in awe of the quiet of the crowd. Everyone seems to be praying; some people are kneeling and sitting, while others are standing with their eyes

Yoshi of Bethlehem

lifted towards the heavens. I am both intent on capturing the spiritual moment and following the priests and the priests-in-training. One of those priests-in-training is Amariah, as he stands among the others on the steps of the Temple, in stillness and reverence.

Amariah told us that Zachariah was one of his mentors at school. That makes this more awesome, but he has been a very long time in executing his duties… Amariah told us what to expect, and this is now at least twice the time that he has spent in the holy place…

With Zachariah's detainment in Temple, I think back to a couple weeks ago. I remember how our presence in Jerusalem came to be.

Joseph and I were tending the sheep in a pasture area where rocks were scattered so much that we found it nec-essary to move the flock each day. Moving daily provided a fresh area to graze, but this made the night-watch more difficult as we had no pen in which to keep the sheep togeth-er safely. Thus, night watch for me was ever so daunting: the days were spent with grazing in place but scouting ahead for the next day's move to fresh grass and then a move each morning to the next field.

It was late afternoon on this day, and I had captured a mourning dove in my basket trap. This would make a nice meal for Joseph and me. I was tired, hungry, and weary of the heavy rain that was falling now for the third day. The rain soaked our firewood, and it took much longer to get a fire started. I thanked God for His provision, as I set about making a fire. Joseph, also hungry and wet, was skillfully keeping the flock together so I could have no concern for them and deal only with our meal.

In the midst of my fatigue and my dismay over the hesitancy of the wood to take to flame, Lydia arrived. As we are in a field far from our home, Lydia walked most of the day to get to us. She tried to cover herself with an extra scarf, but she, too, is drenched from the rain.

"Lydia," I exclaim with great surprise, "how wonderful to see you!"

"And it is wonderful for me as well."

Lydia continues looking toward Joseph as she speaks, "Joseph, how you have grown in the months since last seeing you!"

Yoshi of Bethlehem

Joseph finally notices Lydia and moves quickly to her, "Sister, I am soooo glad to see you. You look so much better than my brother!"

Even though Joseph and I are both pleased to see Sister, we are ashamed we have no shelter to offer her except for a small lean-to of boughs which we move with us daily.

"Come, sit here, Lydia," I implore, ignoring Joseph's humor. "It is the driest place, and I will get this fire going shortly."

Lydia seems relieved to sit and to be somewhat out of the rain. I continue working with the fire and finally get a good start.

"Obviously you have come for a reason, Lydia," I intone.

Lydia unfolds her scarf to produce some cheese, figs, pomegranates, and unleavened bread. "For one thing, I was told to bring you these foods."

Joseph and I both set to salivating! It had been many weeks since we had such welcomed food.

"And the next reason is not so good." Lydia's voice drops. "Mother's ill health has worsened. She has taken a cough that will not leave."

"Oh, no," I say.

"Yes," Lydia continues, "her cough makes it hard for her to breathe at times. The physician has not been able to make her better. Also, a family traveling back to Elam from Jerusalem brought word from Uncle Roshan. Amariah is to be part of his first priestly procession. This will take place at a time when Uncle Roshan must travel for his business. He has invited us all to Jerusalem to honor Amariah with our presence for this procession and to see the city."

Lydia further explains, "Father has determined that the year has been good with his sales of figs, pomegranates, and chickens and from the sale of rams for sacrifice."

As she mentions the rams, I think to the five who I had to release recently for this purpose. Although an honor to have them chosen for sacrifice, like my Jerusha who had perished, they seemed dear to me. Joseph, as well, had a little trouble over letting other families on their way to Jerusalem choose our unblemished males for their sacrifices. But we knew in the end, this was one of the privileges of producing such great stock. There could be no higher use for them than in Jerusalem for sacrifice to God!

"So, with Uncle Roshan's invitation, and with Mother's health, and with a threat of increased taxation by the Romans, Father would like to take this season to go to Jerusalem. This may be our mother's final trip," Lydia's voice faltered at this last comment.

"And we would take a sacrifice too?" questioned Joseph.

"Yes, of course," said Lydia. "You two are to choose the lamb."

"Father will find hirelings to care for the sheep. You are to bring the sheep to the home pen and be ready to leave after two Sabbaths."

Lydia, Joseph, and I were excited and suddenly unaware of our weariness, hunger, and discomfort at being wet. Our sister was here, and the news she brought was overwhelming. We had never traveled. In fact, it was very infrequently that we went to our family home or into Bethlehem itself. Shepherds stay with their flock. I accepted this; Amariah had the opportunity to leave because of Uncle Roshan, but I knew my lot would be the care of these beautiful animals for my lifetime.

The fact that Father would hire someone else to care for my sheep was a bit hard to accept. But the thought of seeing Amariah overrode my trepidation.

Sharon Mullen

So many things whirled through my mind that night as I kept watch over the flock! A trip to Jerusalem, the City of David! My David, my hero! And a visit with my brother whom I have not seen for five years…but also an illness had attached itself to my mother. This made me sad; Father would not suggest this trip if he did not fear for Mother's health.

Lydia remained in the field with us for the night. Joseph and I plumped the straw mattress we shared as best we could and placed it near the fire for Lydia.

As I prayed with Joseph and Lydia that night, I uttered a special prayer for Mother's health.

The morning came all too soon. I had kept the fire tended through the night as the rain continued to fall. It appeared that Lydia's clothing had dried some. I was glad she could leave a bit more comfortable than when she had arrived totally wet.

Joseph and I knew the grass could not support the flock another day at this site. So, we knew that we did not have the luxury of spending time with Lydia and that we must move. It was apparent as well she wanted to get home as soon as possible to help Mother. We ate a scant meal of the remaining cheese and unleavened bread Lydia had brought.

Yoshi of Bethlehem

"I will see you soon then," said Lydia.

So, our presence now in Jerusalem was joyful at seeing Amariah but also woeful as Mother's cough seems uncontrollable for her at times. Even today, this once in a lifetime experience of being at Temple and seeing Amariah take his place among the trained and knowledgeable priests means more to me that I can describe. And Mother is missing this, having chosen to remain at Uncle Roshan's house to rest from our journey. I know that if she were feeling as she had in the past, nothing could stop her from being among those in the outer court with these holy proceedings today. Lydia is there.

I am still looking at Amariah, even though he has not moved one thumb-breadth from his position. I have removed myself from Father and Joseph and have inched toward the front of the waiting crowd to get a full view of the Temple. It has been a really long wait in the sun.

As I wait, I am thinking that it was such a pleasure to find Amariah at Uncle Roshan's when we arrived. I am not sure how the news traveled to him that we would be there on that specific day; I think our last sale of a ram to a Rekabite family may have been the connection for the information to be passed. Nonetheless, we arrived and Amariah immediately set about making us comfortable in Uncle's home, which was easy considering all the amenities his home provides. The house itself had two levels! Made of dried bricks and colored like a golden sunset, there were five individual rooms—unheard of in Bethlehem where our house was one large room divided from the side where our animals stayed in cold months. Uncle Roshan even had beds stuffed with feathers with soft woolen blankets—such luxury!

Amariah had slipped into this lifestyle as easily as it was for him to move about our flock so few years ago. His five years here in Jerusalem seem to have made him more outgoing, more sophisticated, and more of a city-dweller type. He has physically grown too, and he has become even more handsome than I remembered him. He makes my chest puff, but I do not wish to have too much pride!

Uncle Roshan would return by week's end; I was personally glad to have time with Amariah alone in Uncle's home.

Suddenly there is movement at Temple. After this much longer time than Amariah had predicted, Zachariah is finally exiting the Temple. My viewpoint is quite clear. He entered tall and straight but is now somewhat hunched and wan. The

priests closest to the door are taking his elbows to help him
walk. What has transpired, I do not know. But I do not sense
that this was the typical exit of the High Priest after his lighting of the incense. It's as if the priests are carrying him. They
move him a short distance from the entrance to Temple.

I am anxious to leave my place to ask Amariah about
Zachariah, but that would have to wait. A crowd of priests
and their much younger subordinates, including Amariah, was
gathering around Zachariah. I could not see Amariah.

Several other younger students of the Law were motioning quiet among the crowd whose whispers and talking were
beginning to create a small stir. This, too, made me feel that
the happenings now were not typical.

We anxiously lingered under the beating sun. Even
though a high holy experience, the wait in the sun parched my
throat, made my body moist, and caused me to question how
much longer the incense-lighting ceremony would take. The
priestly group with Zachariah seemed to be in discussion.
At one point it appeared that Zachariah had regained his
ability to stand and was flailing his arms and then lifting them
heavenward. The priests and students were gathered quite
some time with him, and I could see that he was writing on a

tablet and showing that to the others. Finally, the entourage with Zachariah began to disperse. The priests went back into their ranks as they followed Zachariah off of the Temple proper. After this procession, the crowd of worshipers started to reverently file out of the area as well. This indicated my need to find my family, including Amariah. He had told us where to wait for him.

As I moved with the crowd towards the outer gate and the tree under which Amariah had told us to wait, my mind was still questioning just what had happened with Zachariah. It seemed an odd occurrence, but who was I to ask this? And what might Amariah know; in fact, where had he been when Zachariah was surrounded by the group of priests?

Amariah was actually waiting for us at the appointed tree.

"Amariah, do you know what happened today?" I asked. "Does the High Priest always become so weak and need help when leaving Temple? Does he always stop and hold a discourse after the lighting of incense? It seemed this took much longer than you had told us."

"My father, brothers, and sister," Amariah started, "this was an extraordinary day at Temple. God has surely proven

Yoshi of Bethlehem

Himself real today. Zachariah was visited by an angel of God as he performed his duties."

My father and I let out an audible gasp at the same time. "Ooooooh."

Amariah looked around as if to make certain no one else was listening.

"I know that Zachariah could not speak when he left the Temple, and he was so weak that he could barely stand. The priests removed him a distance from the Temple entrance. I was not certain of protocol at that point, but I moved in with the priestly crowd. Zachariah motioned for the priests to bring him a writing tablet. He told the other priests that he had been visited by this angel while in the Holy Place. He was lighting incense as his duty instructed, and there was an angel there on the right side of the altar. The angel spoke to Zachariah and told him his prayer had been heard. This angel went on to tell him that he would have a son and that he should name him John. And the angel told him that this son would be a light to many and that he will prepare the way for our Lord, the Messiah!"

Amariah paused here for a moment. It seemed he was searching for just the right words to say or was still overcome with emotion from all that Zachariah had experienced. "Since I have been under the tutelage of Zachariah who is upright and serves the Lord continually, I know that he and his wife, Elisabeth, have prayed many years for a child, a son. In fact, it was a longstanding prayer for him and his wife, who are both now advanced in years. For this today, it is prophetic. Our Messiah is close. How long Israel has waited for this deliverance!"

"For unto us a child is born, unto us a son is given…" Father intoned. "Let me live to see The Messiah."

I was mesmerized by Amariah. Once a shepherd like me, he was truly now dedicated to the service of the Lord and spoke like someone who had studied and believed The Prophecy of a Messiah. It sent a shiver through me. Grandfather wanted to see and to know this day when The Prophecy was coming to pass.

"But there is more. Zachariah cannot speak now. It was a sign given him by the angel of the Lord. When the angel told Zachariah that he and Elisabeth would have a son, Zachariah asked him, 'How can this be?' And the angel gave his name, Gabriel. Gabriel told Zachariah that he stands before the Lord and was sent to give him the news of a son. And he told

Yoshi of Bethlehem

Zachariah that because he doubted that he would not be able to speak until the time of the child's birth. What has been done today sets in motion The Prophecy of old. I am in awe. And to think, you, my family were here to be part of this! May our God be praised."

Chapter 8: Sacrifice

Amariah was right in advising us to arrive "early" the next day to the Temple area for sacrifice. It seems Jerusalem has a different means of keeping time, as this "early" time was typically well past the start of our days in Bethlehem, Joseph and I in the fields, Lydia working in the house, and Father with his fowl and gardens. We all rouse ourselves well before the sun's rays hit our beloved Bethlehem. But here on Temple grounds, there were already families, some who had arrived the day before and were camped out, before us in the queue to sacrifice.

We had passed the Temple market area where animals for sacrifice could be purchased and walked through the central gates. But we were stopped in the Court of the Gentiles by the already-formed line of other Jews waiting to present their offering to God.

Lydia joined us this day, but she would wait in prayer in The Court of the Women. Women did not pass further than that area located towards the entrance. This courtyard area contained many beautiful columns which were part of the Temple proper's structure, and it had beautiful stonework as a flooring. We passed other women already there; ostensibly they, too, were in prayer and waiting for their male family members to return from the sacrifice. It was a family's honored and sacred day, The Day of Atonement. This was the day each year that individual and familial sins could be cleansed.

As Moses set forth by God, each family or individual was bringing their offering. The very poor had brought doves or pigeons; we could hear them squawking even though we could not see them, since it was still dark. We were blessed to bring a ram. Eating meat in Bethlehem was uncommon; it was an overtly expensive endeavor to eat the animals you were raising to sell. Very special occasions such as weddings could mean a family in town would slay an animal for its meat. But generally, meat was not a staple on poor families' plates, and we are considered poor—especially by the standards around Jerusalem! However, at times we would eat fowl that was permitted under the Law (no birds of prey). Father might use one of his fowl at a religious holiday for the family. Joseph and I would keep a trap set in the fields, and we would always feel exceptionally blessed when we caught a bird or small animal that we could cook for meat.

Before leaving the fields for this venture, Joseph and I had chosen our most precious ram for this sacrifice, Jonas. We could offer no less to God. We had discussed this while choosing our best animal, and we both came to the conclusion that Jonas was by far the most handsome and healthy of the flock. He had no blemish that we could find. In preparation for our sacrifice today, Joseph, Amariah, and I had gone out into the dark of the evening last night and picked clean Jonas' fur and even washed him. We knew it was important to offer nothing less than perfection to Him, the Holy One of Israel!

Morning was just breaking into a soft light, and sounds were now emanating from behind the wooden gated area, The Priests' Court, where the sacrifices are made. We could smell the familiar odor of wood fires being stoked. It seemed as if the other families around us were also hearing the movement and now stirring themselves, especially those who were ahead of us and had been in place for the night.

Jonas had chosen this time to relieve himself. I looked at Amariah with a "what-do-we-do" face.

I had not even uttered the question about how to clean up when two very young boys, about the age I was when I began as a shepherd, came seemingly from the shadows. They had wooden instruments and straw and immediately cleared this. They then kept walking down the line; evidently, this was their work.

As they walked away, Amariah broke the silence with, "And thus you have seen one of my first duties when I arrived in Jerusalem and began my priestly studies."

We all smiled.

As the gates of the courtyard of sacrifice opened, our line moved slowly forward. We neared the entrance and were the next family unit in line when a priest came and asked our clan name, city, and type of sacrifice. And very soon after, it was our turn to enter this sacred area with Jonas.

The Priests' Court was magnificently adorned with columns and intricate stonework. The steps leading to the Temple sanctuary were on one side of us, and before us was the altar for the ceremonial offering. Many beautifully crafted metal and clay pots and pans were stacked neatly in rows. These would be used in the collection of blood and animal parts throughout the day, I deducted. In the center was a

Yoshi of Bethlehem

large laver filled with water, and beyond were multiple other washing vessels, all used in the sacrificial offering process.

The blood is the means of atonement for our sins. The priest asked us each to put our hands on Jonas while he prayed for the transference of any sin we carried upon the animal to be sacrificed. He then took our ram and swiftly and effortlessly cut his throat. It was seemingly painless to Jonas, as he simply slumped in sleep. His blood was drained into pans while he hung from a hook. There were younger men with the older priest. It was they who moved a full container and placed another empty one under Jonas lifeless form.

The priest prayed over the family yet another time. His words for removal of all sin from our family, known and un-known, and continued blessing for us were pleasant and spiri-tually cleansing. He prayed and worked on separating parts of the ram.

Ultimately, the priest would take the blood and sprinkle it on the base of the altar of burnt offering. This burning of the blood was the permanent removal of sin. Jonas' fat parts would be burned in one area, and his body would be cooked in another.

Sharon Mullen

The priest reminded us that it was the blood, the life-giving blood for the animal that would be the cleansing aspect for our individual sins and any collective family sins. This blood was the requirement for atonement.

As I stood this day again on the Temple grounds with the priest before us, I recalled the events of yesterday and the wonderful hope that was awakening within my soul. The Messiah. What would His coming mean for us? For our traditions and religious rituals such as this?

The Messiah. Amariah, too, was beside himself with anticipation from the events with Zachariah. But we would need to exercise patience, he had told me last night, as we cleaned Jonas and discussed every nuance of yesterday's events. We had no clear indication how the child that Zachariah has been promised would be used to usher in the Messiah. But we had the promise. We could live with that thought as we waited in faith to see Messiah.

For me today, I walked from the Temple grounds better understanding how my work in the fields of Bethlehem, so far removed from Jerusalem, helped others who purchased our blemish-free animals for their sacrifices. The blood that flowed through them was the important factor in the process

Yoshi of Bethlehem

of cleansing. I knew that from being taught in the Law by Grandfather and Father, but being part of a family sacrifice today at Temple helped me spiritually understand this better. I also walked away with a renewed desire to do my best for God. Most of all, I walked away feeling cleansed.

We stopped for Lydia and ventured on. It seemed we all had our own spiritual thoughts coursing through our minds as we walked back silently through Jerusalem to Uncle Roshan's. Around us, Jerusalem was fully alive and noisy, yet we ambled along quite contentedly not conversing. In fact, we spent most of that day in silent reverence and awe as we prepared for Sabbath the next day.

Chapter 9: Market

Amariah woke us early to visit the market in Jerusalem. Father and Joseph seemed as eager as I for the day ahead of us. Mother was to remain at Uncle Roshan's due to her continued deep and unremitting cough, and thus Lydia stayed to care for her.

We arose and ate leftover bread. This bread was different than ours in Bethlehem and quite delicious. It had been sweetened with honey and dates grown somewhere in Arabia. Just the thought that it was made from foreign foods intrigued me! We then gathered our few coins and our water pouches—now filled with grape juice since we could not drink the water in Jerusalem—and set out as the sun began its morning greeting here in the City of David.

How glad we were immediately that Amariah knew his way through the oft times dark and winding streets! Even without the sun being fully risen, the dusty streets were filling with people. Amariah had said that the Lower City in Jerusalem rises early to begin the workday.

Here in the Lower City, most people are poor manual laborers. There were some who are wealthier from skilled trades, like Uncle Roshan. But most are the poorest of Jerusalem's citizenry. The laborers work in fields outside of the city or in smith shops or work building or repairing carriages and other Roman tools, or as carpenters, potters, bakers. Many doors were already open, revealing shops inside with men already at their tasks. I personally would have found it interesting to enter one of the shops, but Amariah was keen on getting to the market early since it could get very crowded with vendors and buyers.

How exciting for me to be with my favorite men going to market!

"Amariah, how much further?" Joseph asked after we had walked a good distance. The sun was now truly greeting the day with its rays starting to glare at us. This was a different walk than with our sheep. At least with the sheep, we often took shelter from the sun and were walking on earth; here there were no trees under which one could find relief from the

Yoshi of Bethlehem

sun, and the soft earth of our fields was replaced with hardened mud and stone walkways.

"It is honestly not much farther," Amariah continued, "you will know by the air when we are near."

With those few words out of his mouth, I immediately had a cloud of something pleasant sprinkled with the not-so-pleasant descend on me. As we advanced, the smells became stronger. The pleasant smell, I could not decipher; the unpleasant, definitely animals and animal dung!

"Ayyyy, yayyyy!" Joseph exclaimed.

"Yes, you understand what I meant now, don't you?"

Father, typically the quiet one, now spoke up, "I believe I am smelling many, many animals."

"Indeed!" said Amariah. "Camels, cows, sheep, and donkeys. All at market and all for sale."

"I'm just glad our flock does not ever smell like this!" interjected Joseph.

"But, Amariah," I said. "I also smell something sweet. And it is heavily mixed in with the animal odor. If I could smell only that sweet odor, it would be enjoyable! What is that?"

"Spices. Spices from many places. You can come to market and leave laden with spices from Egypt, from Damascus, from Arabia, even from across the Mediterranean Sea! These spices are used for many things. People use them in cooking, for incense, in refreshing the house, for burial. Spices have untold uses."

I was still thinking about spices as we turned a bend to find a host of people ahead. They were all clamoring for access to a single open gate into the market. Roman soldiers stood guard, just as Amariah had told us to expect. Amariah had already told us not to make eye contact with the Roman soldiers. He told us to move past them at every occasion as quickly as possible and to not look at them.

We shuffled in behind a group whose clothing was not as mended or as worn as Father's, Joseph's, and mine. I was beginning to feel out of place as I glanced about at the finery on the men and women in the crowd. It was probably obvious that we were not from Jerusalem.

"You there," cried one of the soldiers. "Stop."

Since Amariah had told us not to make eye contact, we crept forward with the crowd unsure of just whose attention that guard was trying to get.

"You, stop!" He was close by from the sound of his voice, so we had to look up. His spear tip was pointed at Father.

Yoshi of Bethlehem

"Oh, no," I thought. "What could he possibly want?"

"Yes," replied Father with a shaky voice.

"Where are you from, man?" the soldier snarled.

"Bethlehem."

"And why are you here at this market today? What business do you have?"

"I have come merely to experience the wonder of the market," Father honestly replied, again not looking directly at the soldier.

"I will give you the first experience," said the soldier.

By now, no one in the back of us could move forward, and those who had been in front had scurried into the market through that one open gate. We were definitely being watched by many. My previous embarrassment over our clothing was now exacerbated, but I was more concerned about this soldier's portend with Father. My stomach was beginning to knot.

"You must pay the market tax to enter. We don't want just anyone in this market—especially ragged men from Bethlehem. Maybe you have come to start trouble. I don't know, maybe I should just lock you up now." The guard's spear tip was pushed into Father's robe at his chest.

Father shifted from one foot to the other. He was no doubt feeling harried. Although quiet, Father could come out like a bull when needed. But he knew Amariah had urged caution with the Romans.

The soldier said something to the other soldiers in Latin, and they began to laugh.

I watched Father closely. His face became pale.

"Oh God," I silently prayed, "deliver us!"

"What is the tax?" queried Amariah in Aramaic, with a stern voice.

The soldier previously communicating answered, "Eight denarii."

I thought to myself, "Eight denarii! That's more than Father makes from his sales in a year!" I knew Father did not have money to waste, but Father quickly and discretely secured this amount from his tunic pocket.

"Give it to me," said Amariah.

Amariah quickly put it into the soldier's waiting hand. And with a sweep of his non-ragged cloak, Amariah moved us on. He did not wait for any reaction from the soldiers.

But the soldiers did have a response behind us—a raucous laughter.

Yoshi of Bethlehem

The joy seemed to have been drained from all four of us; I could tell by our now less-enthusiastic gait! We entered the gate to the market having been robbed of what was no doubt most of the money Father had mustered for this special trip.

Amariah kept us moving, past stalls of beautiful materials, past baskets of every size and of many colors, past fruits I could not name but wished I could taste. I had never seen such an array of items—and we had just entered the market!

Amariah stopped us in the doorway of a closed shop. We huddled as he spoke.

"Now you understand how the Romans work," Amariah stated rather emotionless. "They take, take, take and yet feel free to take again! But we cannot permit them to dampen our spirits!" Amariah was being overly cheerful at this point. Perhaps he needed to be convinced of this too.

"This is true," Father spoke up. "The Lord will recompense their evil. I have seen it happen before."

"Father," said Amariah, "I am here because I want you to enjoy the market. I also have some funds that I saved for the time when you, my family, would visit. We will walk through the market with renewed excitement. And we will find something that each of you will leave with."

"And we can find a small gift for Lydia and mother," Father stated. "I will pay for those."

I knew that the Romans must have taken most of Father's savings for him to agree so readily to Amariah's charity. I suspect that Amariah was aware of this, too, as he looked at me with a weak smile.

"Let us continue this day enjoying the market," Amariah said, working to buoy our enthusiasm.

And it was working. We turned from the doorway and made our way into the center area and slowly walked the market. I tried to take in every color, every smell, and every nuance of this amazing place. Yes, it was hot and malodorous, but it was wonderful. All the sights and delicious aromas and wonderful foods we were able to taste were more than I could have imagined. Market in Bethlehem was certainly different than this!

My one reflection to Amariah during the day was that the women at market—the Jews—were now wearing a type of veil that covers their hair only; they were showing much of their face with the use of this veil. Of course, Lydia wore that type of veil when with family, but in public she would normal-

Yoshi of Bethlehem

ly be covered. I found this strangely progressive—even for Jerusalem!

Amariah, as he promised, did purchase something for each of us. What was interesting to me is the ease with which he haggled with the merchants. Amariah had certainly been versed by Uncle Roshan in his dealings with merchants! Father chose a leather money pouch; Joseph was thrilled with a wooden game, although when he would have time for that when we were back in the fields in Bethlehem, I was not sure. Perhaps I was being a bit too pragmatic! My choice was a pair of leather sandals, the likes of which I had never seen. They seemed to be custom-made to fit my weary shepherd's feet. The merchant touted their ability to be dry during rain due to a smooth substance that had been rubbed on them. I wore them from that moment forward! I was so thankful to Amariah for their comfort!

Father wanted to purchase mother and Lydia some fine material for dresses, but Amariah convinced him not to do so. Amariah felt that Uncle Roshan, upon his return, would no doubt offer the ladies something from his tailor shop. So, Father purchased hair keepers for them, supposedly made from the ivory of an Egyptian elephant's tusk.

Despite the Romans, we had a tremendous time. That is, until we passed by a stall selling animals. For there on the far side of the stall being led by a mouthpiece was the donkey of Uncle Dathan of Bethlehem! There could be no mistake. The markings on the animal's face could not have been duplicated. There was the sun shining in its glory on the beast's head!

"Father," I cried, "look!" I pointed to the donkey as it was being led from the pen opposite us.

"It is Uncle Dathan's donkey. We must find it…" Father uttered these words as we ran around the pen to where the donkey had been.

Gone.

I cannot explain the speed by which the beast was there and then had vanished into the thick crowd. But the creature being led from the pen was gone in the few paces it took us to arrive there.

Father and I tried to run through the area where the donkey had been spotted and led away. But the crowd seemed even denser at this area; we just could not catch up to it. And we certainly wished to draw no attention to ourselves with Roman guards stationed in the marketplace.

Yoshi of Bethlehem

Amariah knew we were desperate. We had needed to return a donkey to Uncle Dathan. It had already been weeks since the Romans had absconded with this animal. And now it was here and vanished again!

Father spoke with the merchant who had sold the donkey. The merchant, a one-eyed man, said the donkey was weak. He had purchased it from a Roman slave boy and had nursed it from the brink of death back to its current scrawny condition. He had sold the beast for almost nothing to a poor man heading to Nazareth. He was not certain the donkey would even make it that far.

Uncle's donkey was once again outside of our grasp.

"Oh, God," I despaired, "help the donkey to thrive and be useful." Even if we did not have it, at least it would be good for another to have him—and for him to be healthy.

Amariah decided that this was enough "experience" for one day. As we journeyed back toward Uncle Roshan's, we reflected that not only had Father been robbed by the Romans today, but we had once again been reminded that we were previously robbed by the Romans of Uncle's donkey.

But we also jointly discussed and decided again that God is good. As David said, and maybe he spoke this while here in

Jerusalem, "In His Presence is fullness of joy." It was of little consequence to lose the denarii and donkey, we were safely together, and God had provided for us that day. And the Romans could not rob us of our joy.

Chapter 10: School

Today we were going to visit Amariah's school. I was both excited and apprehensive about this visit. I wanted so much to know all about Amariah's life in Jerusalem, which included this school visit, but it also reminded me how much my life's work was considered lower class to the populace in this bustling city.

Making it easy to rise for this day, too, was the thought that Uncle Roshan was to return from his travels from Tyre. His textiles and tailor shop required that he travel to purchase only the best fabrics possible for his clients. His travels also provided that he would see the latest fashion which to tailor in his shop. And Tyre was a great seaport city. Amariah explained that the Romans moved goods from Rome and the mainland to Tyre to be moved again to Lebanon or other parts of Syria and Phoenicia.

Sharon Mullen

My older brother knew so much more about the world than I, now living with Uncle Roshan in Jerusalem. Although his shop is attached to his house in the Lower City, many from the Upper City purchase from Uncle Roshan. It was no wonder he could afford his luxurious home and shop while also providing substantial finances for Amariah's studies.

Soldiers and high-ranking Romans, Israel's socially, politically and religiously elite, as well as some financially upcoming commoners all purchased their clothing from Uncle Roshan. Several people had called to him while we were in the house during our stay, even though the shop was closed, indicating to us that he did not want for customers for which to sew. According to Amariah, Uncle Roshan had a reputation for fine clothing-making, and he charged very fine prices as well!

Uncle Roshan himself is a fascinating study. He had grown up in Bethlehem in my mother's father's home, but he was of different ilk than the other family and friends around him. While helping with his father's small tailor shop in Bethlehem, and learning the skills to sew, Uncle Roshan would wander about the immediate region seeking better fabrics and investigating the clothing of the wealthy. He also did business from his father's shop with non-Jews. This was not viewed

Yoshi of Bethlehem

very favorably by other Jews and the priests and elders. Yet Uncle Roshan did this with impunity!

I knew that Father, Amariah, and Joseph were waiting for me. But today I wanted to look my very best to go to Amariah's school where we would meet his teachers and other students. I did not want to disappoint or embarrass Amariah. I tried to trim and scrub myself and refresh my tunic and robe with a sprinkle of water here and there, but try as I did, it was futile. I still looked the part of a shepherd from Bethlehem. At least my sandals were new-from-market-in-Jerusalem!

I was descending the stairs when I heard a commotion; it was Uncle Roshan with his travel/tailoring assistant! They had returned. Uncle was exuberant at seeing all of us—as we were to see him. He motioned to his assistant who quickly left.

Lydia had prepared a morning meal, and as we ate, we took the opportunity to share the events of the past couple of days with Uncle Roshan. From the report of the robbery of Father's money, and the missing donkey showing up at market, to the most spectacular: that of Priest Zachariah and his prophecy of Messiah. Telling about the Temple visit again brought awe over all of us as we reclined at the table.

This pause of reflection and awe was broken by the return of Uncle Roshan's assistant. His arms were laden with clothing.

"It must be what Uncle Roshan has purchased while away and he wants to show us," I mused. And I could see splendid looking apparel neatly stacked over his arm!

"Today is your visit to the school, correct?" asked Uncle Roshan looking at Amariah.

"Indeed, Uncle," said Amariah, "we planned to leave soon after the morning meal."

"Very well then," he said. "I have something for each of you. Those visiting the school may wish to change."

And with that, the assistant—who was not introduced but I certainly wondered where he was from as he did not look like a Jew—began to place items in each of our laps or behind us as we reclined. He knew who would receive which outfit.

I had been facing the table, so when I turned around to see what had been placed by me, I could not believe it. There was a new undergarment, tunic, leather belt, and outer robe the color of the soft desert sands in Bethlehem. It was fetching. As I touched it, I realized it was the most finely spun wool I had ever felt. There was a finely embroidered neck with tassels at the corners of the robe as prescribed by Jewish custom.

My father and Joseph had outfits just as smart as mine. Mother and Lydia had finely tailored, soft linen tunics with beautifully embroidered, variously-colored desert flowers on the sleeves with long veils that matched the color of the flowers' stems. There was, however, a difference with their veils. They were designed like those being worn in Jerusalem. Lydia and Mother's faces would not be totally covered in public should they wear these veils.

I was speechless about the receipt of these extravagant clothes. Father was speechless. Mother was speechless but still coughing. Lydia did not speak. Joseph sat dumbly.

In between fits of coughing, Mother finally spoke, "Roshan, how can we accept such expensive gifts? We are not accustomed to such finery. In all my years, Brother, I have never seen such exquisitely tailored robes and tunics. Even wedding raiment in Bethlehem is not so fine as this."

Uncle Roshan got up quickly; he did not want this to be overwhelming to us. He spoke to Amariah, "Take your brothers and change for the school visit. Joel, do you also wish to change?"

"Do you think it best, Roshan?" asked Father.

"Yes," he responded as he gathered Father's clothing pile, "I think you will feel more comfortable in these clothes when going into the Upper City where the school is located. The area is known for its splendor and opulence. The Romans might even stop you again, as they did at the market, in your Bethlehemite apparel. And I know you'd rather not deal with them again!"

Mother and Lydia were to change too. He specifically requested that they wear the veils now in vogue in Jerusalem. Uncle Roshan decided that they would accompany him today to a beautiful garden not far from his home. He had already set up a beast to pick up Mother. And he would dine with them at an inn. Even through her fits of coughing, you could tell Mother was more excited than she had been since our arrival.

Uncle Roshan's reputation for tailoring was played out in the garments with which we were adorned as we left his house to walk to the Upper City. As he was also detailed minded, he had leather sandals in great supply for each of us to find a fitting pair to go with our new robes. I truly did not want to remove the pair I had just purchased at the market, but once

Yoshi of Bethlehem

I felt the even finer leather of those Uncle Roshan was offering, I quickly acquiesced.

Father, Amariah, Joseph, and I walked some distance
among the close, sun-burned houses on the dusty streets of
the Lower City. We now looked the part of men from Jerusalem and not shepherds from Bethlehem! Amariah again
proved a great guide as he showed us local points of interest as well as Roman ingenuity. The Romans had installed
an aqueduct along the road we traversed; it was meant to
convey water through the main walking area where Uncle
Roshan's house was located. It had yet to reach Uncle Roshan's house, as its work was not complete, but water flowed
through the tiled channels that were complete. There was
also a Roman amphitheater on our way to the Upper City.
Even at a distance, this was a beautiful structure.

As we ascended the walking road towards the Upper
City, it became wider, cleaner, and paved with sizable, sun-
baked brick. Amariah informed us that this was a Roman
road; some factors made life with these pagans more tolera-
ble, and their road-building was one of those things. I could
understand what he meant by this last comment as the "road"
was actually more easily walked as the bricks were laid quite

evenly and in a very eye-pleasing pattern. Amariah told us that the road would be more of a smooth walk now till arriving at the school.

With every step going to the Upper City the view became more spectacular. There were gardens with beautifully planted flowers and trees as we walked higher and higher, but there was also a view of the Lower City below us. It was as if we were entering another city as we reached the summit. What Amariah failed to tell us is how majestic the homes became at the Upper City!

Below us, the Lower City looked as if a cloud of dust had settled over row after row of tightly packed houses. But here in the Upper City was a broad avenue with multi-storied houses. Not only were the houses large, but they were decorated in manners I had never witnessed. There were white columns and white porches on most of these homes that Amariah told us were made of marble. These houses stretched out like the flock when we reached a heavily grassed area and each lamb would find a great swath of grass upon which to feast and recline without coming anywhere near another sheep. And in the space between the houses were beautiful gardens and tall statues and foaming fountains. Joseph and

Yoshi of Bethlehem

I could have grazed the flock for a day on the grassy area between the houses! The noisy clatter of life and the filth of the stirred-up dust of the Lower City were replaced with a calm and very clean atmosphere. Even the people walking on the road seemed less frenetic, less pressured to get to their destination.

"Welcome to the Upper City," said Amariah.

I'm sure he knew we were mesmerized by the houses and gardens and their grandeur.

"We need to walk some distance further," Amariah continued. "You will find more of these houses as we go. There are no shops within these living areas. They are ahead as we reach the school."

I was suddenly very aware that Uncle Roshan had done us a major favor in providing our new apparel today. A man in traditional, but elaborate, Jewish attire just passed us. The few people we met as we walked in the Upper City were dressed equally as fine. Several Romans on large horses went by. Again, we practiced Amariah's advice of not making eye contact and just kept walking.

We reached a central area which opened to shops. It was apparent that there had been a morning market here that was now folding, but again it was being shut down slowly and quietly. The shops themselves were built much nicer than those in the Lower City. The mud of the Lower City used for the building material was replaced by a more substantial mortar with large rocks or sun-dried brick. I suspected the goods within those shops were also of a higher quality and price than those found in the Lower City as well.

Amariah adjusted his robe and announced that we had arrived. There before us was the school. "School of Law," was the sign on the outside of another magnificent looking edifice with white marble pillars on the front.

"Follow me, please," said Amariah as we entered the quiet building. "Please wait for me here. I will return shortly."

Once my eyes adjusted from having been in the sun, I could tell we were in a large room with wooden seating. I could also discern from the outset that the school was going to be as grand as the homes we had witnessed on our walk.

Two young boys in very drab apparel appeared from a door on the opposite side of the room. They came bearing a basin and towels and motioned for us to be seated. They then washed our feet, eldest to youngest.

Yoshi of Bethlehem

Amariah returned with his Jewish mentor, a man named Gamaliel. He was older, a bit bent and wore frontlets. Uncle Roshan and Amariah had already told us of Gamaliel. He was a very celebrated Doctor of Mosaic Law and was President of the Sanhedrin. We were introduced by Amariah. I felt it strange that a teacher of such renown would be such a wisp of a man physically.

He spoke a few words to Father with such a soft voice that, try as I might, I could not make out their conversation.

The only snatch of conversation between them that I caught was at the end of a thought and was Gamaliel saying, "….yes, I am sorry that you cannot meet Zachariah today. He might have been able to dispel some of your unease."

We were then taken to meet classmates who were in study. Gamaliel explained that they would have a time of refreshing soon when classes were interrupted for a short meal. Gamaliel offered an escort to a small room where a dozen young men the age of Amariah were seated on wooden benches with prayer shawls draped across their shoulders. Gamaliel requested that Amariah take his seat. Each was called on individually to state his name.

Then at Gamaliel's instruction, they collectively quoted Deuteronomy, chapter six.

"Now these are the commandments, the statutes, and the judgments, which the Lord your God commanded to teach you, that ye might do them in the land whither ye go to possess it:

That thou mightest fear the Lord thy God, to keep all his statutes and his commandments, which I command thee, thou, and thy son, and thy son's son, all the days of thy life; and that thy days may be prolonged.

Hear therefore, O Israel, and observe to do it; that it may be well with thee, and that ye may increase mightily, as the Lord God of thy fathers hath promised thee, in the land that floweth with milk and honey.

Hear, O Israel: The Lord our God is one Lord:

And thou shalt love the Lord thy God with all thine heart, and with all thy soul, and with all thy might.

And these words, which I command thee this day, shall be in thine heart:

And thou shalt teach them diligently unto thy children, and shalt talk of them when thou sittest in thine house, and when thou walkest by the way, and when thou liest down, and when thou risest up.

And thou shalt bind them for a sign upon thine hand, and they shall be as frontlets between thine eyes.

And thou shalt write them upon the posts of thy house, and on thy gates.

And it shall be, when the Lord thy God shall have brought thee into the land which he sware unto thy fathers, to Abraham, to Isaac, and to Jacob, to give thee great and goodly cities, which thou buildedst not,

And houses full of all good things, which thou filledst not, and wells digged, which thou diggedst not, vineyards and olive trees, which thou plantedst not; when thou shalt have eaten and be full;

Then beware lest thou forget the Lord, which brought thee forth out of the land of Egypt, from the house of bondage."

At this point, the oral reading returned to the first student who continued with the next verse:

"Thou shalt fear the Lord thy God, and serve him, and shalt swear by his name.

Ye shall not go after other gods, of the gods of the people which are round about you;

(For the Lord thy God is a jealous God among you) lest the anger of the Lord thy God be kindled against thee, and destroy thee from off the face of the earth.

Ye shall not tempt the Lord your God, as ye tempted him in Massah.

Ye shall diligently keep the commandments of the Lord your God, and his testimonies, and his statutes, which he hath commanded thee.

And thou shalt do that which is right and good in the sight of the Lord: that it may be well with thee, and that thou mayest go in and possess the good land which the Lord sware unto thy fathers.

To cast out all thine enemies from before thee, as the Lord hath spoken.

And when thy son asketh thee in time to come, saying, What mean the testimonies, and the statutes, and the judgments, which the Lord our God hath commanded you?

Then thou shalt say unto thy son, We were Pharaoh's bondmen in Egypt; and the Lord brought us out of Egypt with a mighty hand:

Yoshi of Bethlehem

And the Lord shewed signs and wonders, great and sore, upon Egypt, upon Pharaoh, and upon all his household, before our eyes:

And he brought us out from thence, that he might bring us in, to give us the land which he sware unto our fathers.

And the Lord commanded us to do all these statutes, to fear the Lord our God, for our good always, that he might preserve us alive, as it is at this day.

And it shall be our righteousness, if we observe to do all these commandments before the Lord our God, as he hath commanded us."

My Father kept wiping his eyes as they recited. A heavenly chorus could not have been more in tune.

Each student sat at his bench upon completion of the last verse. Gamaliel then gave them leave.

"Amariah, you have made me proud," said Father, as Amariah returned to our family group. "That was beautiful."

Amariah thanked him and ushered us from the room. He moved us toward a large portico (a word he had taught us) where the young men were gathering at tables with fruit arranged for their taking.

A young man, maybe a year or two younger than Amariah, came to us. "Please, I want to meet your family, Amariah," he said.

"Father, Joseph, Yoshi, I would like you to meet Phillip. Phillip is from Tarsus but grew up in Jerusalem. He is my best friend."

And with that introduction, I met Amariah's "best friend." It struck me as a bit unfortunate that I was no longer being recognized in the role of "best friend," even though as brothers we had been best friends for many years.

But this Phillip was quite honestly the most good-looking young man I had ever met. With dark curly hair and fine features, it was clear that he was a Jew from another country. Although several years younger, Amariah told us later that he was such an exceptional student of the Law that Phillip was educated by Gamaliel at an advanced pace. He was now in studies with Amariah.

Gamaliel called to Phillip who bowed and excused himself.

The opulence of the facility, the stark splendor of the polished furniture, and the wisdom that flowed from Gamaliel and other instructors I met made me more aware of how uncomfortable I was in this place where Amariah now found such ease to move about and be educated. As much as I had wanted to physically be present in the school because it had pertinence to Amariah, I was now anxious to take leave.

"Oh, God, help me," I said to myself. "I feel like one of the lambs who has been trapped in an unfamiliar yet cool and comfortable cave. I'd like to relax and enjoy this, but it's too unfamiliar; I know I cannot stay here forever to glean from Scripture as Amariah has."

Amariah showed us further through the school while the break was occupying the students. There were several rooms outfitted as the first. There was a grassy area with several benches where contemplation could take place. And there was a cooking area that Lydia and Mother would have loved to use! I imagined Amariah as he came here initially as an older student than the very young boys who had washed our feet; it must have been challenging to him to have to catch up with those in his age group.

Our return trip to Uncle Roshan's was another breath-taking walk. Amariah took a different footpath, one that Jews typically use. This path also afforded us a panoramic view of the Lower City with the Temple rising further above us in the distance with each step downward until we could glimpse it no more for the trees.

The night and noise of the Lower City descended on us as we walked in a line due to the steep and rocky trail. My thoughts were on my hero David. I wondered to myself how often he had walked on a path such as this. Jerusalem was not the small city it was when David was king, but I could imagine still his presence in this beautiful place, and it was easy for me to understand how he could have written so many songs while living in this great city as he sought to serve the Lord.

That night at prayer, Father quoted some of David's words, "The Lord is my rock and my fortress and my deliverer! I will call upon the Lord who is worthy to be praised."

I drifted to sleep thinking how God is to be praised for what He has done for all of us in our family!

Chapter 11: Lydia

The sounds of the early morning awoke me; roosters could be heard in rolling swells from one end of Jerusalem to the other, interspersed with babies and young children softly crying here and there; no doubt they wanted their mothers and their next meals. Amariah was not on his side of the finely feathered mattress we shared during our visit. As I arose, I was again at awe over the sheer magnificence of such a sleeping pad and its finely woven cover. I was reminded anew that I was not in the fields in Bethlehem on my straw mat!

I dressed quietly in my old robe and went up to the rooftop to find Amariah in his prayer vigil; I had found him here on other occasions in the morning during our time at Uncle's. His prayer shawl was loosely draped across his shoulders, and he was seated in such a way that he appeared a Goliath of a man physically. And truly in my estimation, Amariah was a Goliath; he had killed many a giant to battle the move from our tiny town of Bethlehem to being victorious in the knowledge of the ways of a large city like Jerusalem. Moreover, he had taken the biblical teaching received at home by Grandfather and Father and had amplified that from his current studies and hard work at The School of Law and from his own studies and personal relationship with God.

I sat down on a tufted pad not far from Amariah, hoping I was not interrupting his personal prayer time. I joined him in silent prayer as he uttered my favorite Psalm:

"...yea though I walk..." Amariah reverently spoke.

In my mind, I was thanking God as I remembered how that Psalm of David has been a comfort to me on several levels and on many occasions! I thought specifically of my sheep and acknowledged my trust in God that they were being well tended now. And I thought of the many times the Lord was my Shepherd and guided me as I pastored the flock and led them on paths which could at times be dangerous.

I must have dozed off, for when I awoke, Joseph and Father were also present and talking with Amariah. The subject was again the visit to Temple.

Yoshi of Bethlehem

Father was speaking, "And you know Zachariah well? And you believe him to be a holy priest?"

"Yes, quite well, Father..." Amariah's response was cut short.

Suddenly there was a huge commotion below at the closed doorway to Uncle Roshan's shop. He had left yesterday afternoon for his business and would not be back until evening today. For the past few days we had been present in Jerusalem, there had been no one calling. With Uncle Roshan out, Amariah got up to investigate the commotion. I decided to follow.

With the lifting of the wooden arm at the shop's entrance door, the door swung wide open, creaking loudly as if to echo the garish talking outside. The cause of the commotion at once became evident, for there was a group of Roman soldiers gathered at the door with several chariots stationed just beyond them.

"Of course," I thought, "they think they own Jerusalem and can be obnoxious anywhere and at any time."

"Good day, men," said Amariah, unfazed by their number (I quickly counted six) or their uniforms, "I want to let you know that Roshan will not be available today."

107

"No, that is unacceptable," exclaimed one of the six, "for he was to complete a garment for me today."

I craned my neck to see the soldier speaking. He was bronzed from the sun and wore the typical Roman soldier attire of a short tunic with a metal breastplate, but his helmet held a large reddish-purple tall plume. None of the others' headgear had such a look.

"He will return this evening," offered Amariah.

The soldier with the plumage spoke again. "Roshan told us he would be here today. I need the tunic today."

"I am sorry for this miscommunication, but Roshan nor his assistant will be in the shop today. You will need to return in the morning."

"I need it now," he insisted. "Can we come in and look for it? With all of us looking," he continued with a sneering tone, "we can find it—or tear the place apart looking!!"

The group was amused by his smirky comment and gave up some laughs.

It appeared that Amariah was not totally unaccustomed to rudeness. He did not flinch as he responded to them, "You need to return tomorrow."

Yoshi of Bethlehem

"Nooooooo," exclaimed the plumaged-helmet soldier. "We do not have time to return. I must have this garment to-day."

"Roshan will return by evening. We are unable to assist you now." Amariah stated this with no room for discussion.

The five Roman soldiers deferred to the plumaged-helmet one; they waited for his response.

"We will return tomorrow. Good day."

Amariah motioned me back, swiftly closed the door, and dropped the wooden latch to secure entry to the shop once again.

"They can return when Uncle Roshan is here," said Amariah, seemingly unruffled by the group at the door. "That has been our customary response when anyone comes and Uncle Roshan or Ketab are not present."

We returned to Father and Joseph on the rooftop. The sun was beginning to heat up all of Jerusalem; we took refuge in the shade of the tall potted plants Uncle Roshan keeps on the roof. Lydia was working with a servant girl in preparing the morning meal. The oven fire burned in one corner with the smell of bread wafting towards us. Today was to be one of leisure and walking near Uncle Roshan's house and shop.

And it proved to be an enjoyable, albeit lazy day with my family.

The evening meal was a welcomed occasion for my very empty stomach. Lydia quietly sought me out afterward and asked me to meet her in Uncle Roshan's shop when all had retired.

With the sounds of sleeping in the air, and darkness having fallen, I quietly slipped from the room with Amariah and Joseph into Uncle's shop. It seemed strange to enter it without his knowledge, but I found Lydia already there awaiting me with a small lamp that obliterated the total obscurity of the shop.

"She must have something important to discuss," I thought to myself. "She would not have asked for me to come in stealth in the night."

"Yoshi," Lydia began as soon as I entered, "thank you for coming. I need to talk to you and to tell you about a new friend."

The word "friend" caught my attention. I had not heard the word from her uttered in this manner. I didn't know why, but I could immediately ascertain that this was a male "friend." Lydia was beautiful and good; her goodness caused her to care more about others than herself. But she was past the typical age where marriages are either firmly arranged or already consummated. I had actually wondered—no, worried—for her since her time in Bethlehem had always been spent helping Mother. She did not mingle with those in the village, and there were few males, if any, whose family might find her a fitting marriage partner. There had only been the one young man whose life was cut short by the Romans…

Lydia broke my contemplation with, "I will tell you directly, it is a man, and he is Roman."

"Oh, a Roman, Lydia?" I let that out before thinking. I should let her do all the speaking!

"But a Roman???" I was thinking to myself! "These are the people we detest! People who murdered your husband!"

"Yes. You remember that yesterday Mother and I went with Uncle Roshan to the Gardens of Gerbesh? Uncle Roshan had hired a beautiful horse-drawn carriage to take Mother to the garden while we walked beside her. We stayed several hours in the gardens. It was a magnificent place with white marble statues and delightful flowers I had never seen from lands I never knew existed! Uncle Roshan then had the carriage take Mother to a nearby inn where we ate. It was quite an exciting experience, first the gardens and then a meal at such a place. And Mother's cough was under control for most of the day! After our delicious meal, we went back outside for Mother to once again be seated for the ride home, but the horse and its owner were gone. Uncle Roshan was so angry. The inn manager told us to walk about five furlongs and we would find another stable shop where they rented horses and camels too. Mother said she could walk that far so that we would not need to return to the inn after getting another horse carriage. We ambled along and arrived at the stable he indicated, but they had no beasts available. By this time, Mother was coughing from the dust blowing up from the street, I believe."

"Oh, no," I said, unsure where all this discourse was leading.

"Yes. Uncle Roshan was not totally familiar with the area we were in as far as available beasts of burden. The stable hand suggested that he speak to a family not far from the shop to ask about their horse and carriage. Again, Mother heard this conversation and stated that she could walk that far. But Mother was already in a coughing state. I knew she could not walk much more. Uncle Roshan was aware of

Yoshi of Bethlehem

that as well. We had left the stable and were ever more slowly walking toward the house the stable hand had pointed
out. Mother was coughing and stumbled on a loose stone
and fell. It was terrible… except for the next part. A Roman
dressed in a very fancy uniform with an amazing helmet with a
purple plume was passing; he rode in a shiny chariot with the
most splendid horse. He saw Mother's fall. I saw him look at
us. He turned his horse and chariot back to us, and I wondered," said Lydia, "if he was returning to be cruel to Mother.
I jumped in front of her to shield her from him. But he was
different than my first evaluation of the Romans. Yoshi, he
was so handsome and kind and handsome and careful with
mother and handsome. Did I mention he was handsome? His
facial features were nothing like the Jewish men I know. He
had small features and eyes the color of what I imagine the
Mediterranean Sea is. And he really was kind! He asked
Uncle Roshan if he could help, and Uncle Roshan immediately
told him, 'yes' and asked him to let Mother ride in his chariot
to Uncle Roshan's home."

"Lydia, was he handsome?" I asked with a loose smile she
probably could not see in the light of her small lamp.

"Yoshi, I was able to ride in the chariot as well. He and Uncle Roshan walked along talking the whole trip home. Their banter made it seem as if they had known each other. I wanted so badly to hear their words! When we arrived here, he took my hand and helped me down. He then asked me, by name—I'm sure he had asked Uncle Roshan for my name—if I would like to join him tomorrow with friends, a married couple, to see a Roman chariot race. Uncle Roshan would be my escort as well. I was dumbfounded and did not know how to respond. He was speaking directly to me! Mother spoke up for me and said I would enjoy that!

"Uncle Roshan asked for the time I should be ready. And just like that, he was gone. I had to ask Uncle Roshan for his name: Marcus Blandus Calvus.

"But here's where I need your counsel, Brother. When Mother told Father about the soldier and that he would be coming for me to leave with him tomorrow—and remember Uncle Roshan is accompanying us—Father was not happy. I was not in the room, but I could hear parts of the discussion and know that Father does not wish for me to be with a 'pagan.' He was quite adamant that I not be seen with this soldier. He further told Mother he did not even trust Uncle

Roshan in the matter. Through bouts of coughing, Mother told Father that Uncle Roshan had no problem with this, and most of Jerusalem would have no problem. Uncle had already told Father that there were many mixed marriages now in Jerusalem and that Herod was encouraging them."

"Oh, Lydia, so Father forbids that you go?" I asked, hopeful that her answer was in the affirmative.

"Yes, but Mother said that the plans had been made."

It dawned on me at that point that the evening meal conversation had been subdued; I had initially suspected that everyone was tired from the day's idleness. "So that's why the meal tonight was so quiet."

"Yoshi, yes, it was my fault."

"No, Lydia, this is not anyone's fault. But what do you intend to do?"

"I have never gone against Father or Mother, but I do wish to know Marcus Blandus Calvus and go to that chariot race. We leave Jerusalem in 4 days; I will never see him again."

Lydia continued, "You see why I could not ask Amariah for an opinion, of course. It would put him in an awkward position with the Jewish leaders at his school and at Temple."

"You are right, Lydia."

"Yoshi, I feel badly that Father is not happy about this." With this statement, I could hear Lydia's voice quiver. "I know this is different than how we know a man and woman meet and talk. But I know the Romans are not all bad…"

"You should ask God what He wants, Lydia." I interrupted not wanting to hear her goodness spill over onto an explanation of the Romans! "What dogs!" was all I could think.

"I know God wants me to be happy. Until today I had never thought that I could hope to have even a male friend. Is it so bad that he is Roman, Yoshi?"

This question made my stomach ache. My sister knew that Father was robbed several days ago at market by a Roman soldier, she knew about the Roman thieves running our flock and causing the death of Jerusha and her lamb, she knew that we were taxed beyond reason by the Romans…she knew Romans were the reason she was unmarried. She knew they were in our country defying our beliefs and destroying our culture. If she could have heard the gall of the group just this morning demanding merchandise we could never find in Uncle Roshan's shop! How could she desire to personally know and be seen with one of these soldiers!

116

Yoshi of Bethlehem

"Yoshi?" repeated Lydia, "is his being Roman such a big issue?"

At this moment, as if by Divine intervention, a cat let out a huge wail and then somehow jumped via a high window into the shop. How this happened, I am not sure, but I was alarmed at the thought of a cat in the midst of all the fine fabric in the shop—and in a shop that we should not be in at the moment either.

"Lydia, we have to get this cat out of the shop," I said, relieved for the disturbance; however, I was trying to keep my voice down to a whisper-with-a-hint-of-panic level.

The cat must have been surprised to hear a human voice, for it immediately sprang back to the window ledge and jumped out onto the neighbor's rooftop. Another scream emanated, and it was gone into the night.

Such a timely interruption! I hoped we would not return to the discussion at hand, but Lydia pressed me, "Yoshi, do you, too, not want me to be friends with Marcus?"

"Marcus? Marcus?" I thought. "Now she's using his name!" I was not pleased with this idea. But how do I tell my dear sister?

"Lydia, I, too, want you to be happy. But I also know that we have always been instructed not to intermarry..." What else could I say? That I loathed the Romans and would rather see her with no male in her life than to be with a Roman!

With that, the lamplight flickered; the oil was drained. I was drained, and I think Lydia was too.

"Thank you for your honesty, Yoshi." Lydia choked out, and she quietly slipped by me.

I was left in the darkness with my dark, ugly thoughts of the Romans. And I was left with disappointment that Sister would be in the company of one of them tomorrow.

I had not moved too far in the shop when I heard voices outside. I was certainly glad that Lydia and I had not spoken above a whisper! I paused in curiosity and heard a bit of the conversation.

"...that is equivalent to a year's salary." said an unknown voice.

"Precisely," said the voice of Uncle Roshan. "But you can make up for that with Herod's dividend."

"I could pay less with Reuben of Tyre," replied the voice again.

Yoshi of Bethlehem

But wait, I had heard this voice before. It was just today in the shop. It sounded like the reddish-purple plumed demanding soldier.

"You are not getting the same quality, my friend," retorted Uncle Roshan. "Think of the known beauty, and the family line. It's like buying a fine ewe. And think of your advancement …"

I was feeling a bit guilty about continuing to listen to the conversation, but it had piqued my interest too much to leave. "Were they talking about robes or textiles or sheep or something else?" I thought, as I continued to stand in place.

"Roshan," interrupted the voice, "you amaze me. Not only are you shrewd at finding the best materials for your shop, but you are also clever at selecting good stock for our business. And to provide such a close one! Roshan, you have no morals!" exclaimed the voice which I still felt had a familiar ring to it.

"What could this mean?" I pondered, but I knew I could not stay or I would risk running into Uncle Roshan who would question my presence. I slipped into the dark house and into the bedchamber.

I lay on the fine mattress next to Amariah, who was thankfully in deep sleep as indicated by soft snoring. I pondered the discussion with Lydia and her mention of the soldier she had met having a purple plume on his helmet. Then I considered the conversation with Roshan and the voice outside just now and wondered if it really could have been the same voice belonging to the Roman soldier with the reddish-purple plumaged helmet I saw this morning at the shop door. Was I simply illogically thinking this soldier could be the same one in all circumstances? How many horse-riding Roman soldiers were there with reddish-purple plumed helmets in Jerusalem now?

And my thoughts jerked back to Lydia and her desire to befriend a Roman. And a Roman soldier at that! "Perhaps," I thought, "this meant less in Roman culture; perhaps it really only means a mere friendship."

I knew that to a Jew, an offer of an outing would indicate relationship interest. Marriage interest. To the Jews, there was no frivolous time spent in outings; a couple became betrothed and worked towards marriage, mostly within a year.

"No, no, no!" was all I could mentally come up with. "She cannot get involved with a Roman, especially not a Roman soldier!"

Yoshi of Bethlehem

But I knew my attitude was not truly good, so as I prayed at that time, I asked God to help me understand the complex situation now facing my family.

"God," I prayed, "may I seek to do good among the evil around me." Ezekiel's words seemed appropriate for this prayer!

Chapter 12:   Return

Joseph and I are now back where we feel very comfortable: in the fields with our flock.   Thankfully, the hirelings tending the flock while we were in Jerusalem were capable and took great care of the sheep. In fact, two young rams had been successfully birthed while we were gone. Often with hirelings, the care rendered is not acceptable; but these shepherds were known to us and proved reliable.

I was on the night watch, sitting under a covering of brilliant stars and thinking back on our happy, yet unhappy, events of the past few weeks. What a delight it had been to be able to witness all the sights and sounds of the city where Amariah was now comfortably ensconced! That was a great pleasure, one which I knew I would not soon enjoy again. Jerusalem, The City of David, was indeed a world of difference from tiny Bethlehem. Amariah was content there amidst the flurry of daily activity with his schooling and his student priestly duties, and I could be quite happy to never again leave my beloved city and my flock. There is always something comforting with the familiar.

Our return trip was hard. Father had woken the family before the morning light the next day after Lydia had attended the chariot race with her Roman friend. (I cannot bring myself to name him!) We were leaving as soon as we could put our belongings together and prepare a light meal for the day's journey. In his voice, there was no hint of the possibility of questioning leaving in such a hurry. We were originally to have remained several more days. To travel this far with Mother's delicate health, but leave in such haste, made me know that Father wanted Lydia out of Jerusalem and far away from all Romans. I knew Father desired Lydia to have no more connection with her new friend who was keen on returning for Lydia to take her to see more of Jerusalem on this day of our hurried departure. Uncle Roshan told me the Roman was to return for Lydia. Uncle seemed quite pleased.

On our return, Mother seemed very subdued but was not coughing as much. Perhaps the time away had been good for her health. Amariah returned to school since we were leaving;

it was indeed a bitter herb to have to say goodbye yet again to my best friend and brother. Uncle Roshan and Ketab walked with us most of the morning, ate lunch with us, but he and the assistant left to return to Jerusalem right after lunch. We watched them as they walked out of sight.

While walking with us, however, Uncle Roshan had used the time to bring up the issue of Lydia having made friends with the Roman soldier. In his indomitable way, he kept the subject from being dropped, as Father attempted. Uncle Roshan offered the opinion that Israel was changing and that the Romans had been ruling so long that many were comfortable with their customs and laws. He discussed their presence throughout Israel and their importance in the arts and society as well as their importance in the establishing of Israel as a useful trade route due to their engineering of roads, viaducts, and other publicly traveled and utilized venues. He was pleased that, for the most part, the Romans left the Jewish religious world to guide and rule in matters of family and tradition as that tradition and our religion dictated.

Uncle Roshan ventured his thoughts that Lydia should have been free to be with Marcus. He also ventured his opinions that the "arranged marriage" custom of the Jews was outdated. Perhaps he was a good suitor for her since her arranged marriage had never been consummated. Uncle Roshan further described his knowledge of their ranks and salaries and discussed how Lydia could be quite comfortable living in the home of a Roman soldier of his stature. He was, after all, a Roman equestrian; this meant his salary was quite high as compared to other soldiers. And, as Uncle Roshan was quick to point out, no ordinary Bethlehemite suitor could match in ten years what Marcus could make in one.

"Roshan, I see no reason whatsoever for my daughter to have anything to do with a Roman, and a Roman soldier makes me twice as certain that there is no 'friendship,' as you call it, warranted." Father snapped at Uncle Roshan. "I really don't care about his salary, nor his position as an equestrian..."

"You, Joel, need to understand the world today. There are many reasons for Lydia to marry a Roman. Our Jewish lives and culture are changing. To marry a Roman, and especially a highly regarded soldier, would bring much prestige to our family. Herod is interested in a mixed-race nation; it would help bring stability and provide financial gain to Israel."

Yoshi of Bethlehem

"There it is, Roshan. The very reason not to mix—we need to remain Jews! We don't need these Romans directing our lives. Herod is subverting the nation, our culture, our religion."

"Herod's reign has done much to better all of Israel. The trade lines, roads, civic facilities, even some religious areas, have been improved. Why …"

"Enough Roshan. You border on blasphemy. We've nothing more to discuss. Rome and its puppets need to leave Israel."

Mother seemed pleased by her brother's insight as I watched her face while Uncle Roshan spoke, but she clouded as Father offered his opines. Lydia seemed uncomfortable and kept walking with her head down and made no comment. I think Joseph and I both felt the same way with this conversation—we'd rather have been in the fields counting sheep. Father's disposition was finally heard when Uncle Roshan made this comment:

"Joel, you might as well embrace the change the Romans bring. They are in Israel to stay."

With indignation in his typically meek voice, Father replied, "Never, Roshan, never." End of discussion.

And with the next bend in the road back to Bethlehem, our world was shattered by the bold reality that we are governed by Rome. There, hanging on a cross beam between two tree trunks was a "thief." His crime was so noted by the sign hanging above which had been written in several languages. He was in agony and bleeding from the wounds in his hands and feet where he had been cruelly pounded onto the tree trunks with large wooden spikes. Roman soldiers stood there laughing and gouging him further with their spears. Mother and Lydia looked away. I wished I had not seen this atrocity either. Uncle Roshan quickened his pace as if to encourage us to get away from the perpetrators of the deed.

"Romans. When Messiah comes," I thought, "He will deliver us from their rule!"

Now we are once again with the flock. And I feel I am where I should be. Joseph and I remained one night in Bethlehem upon our return from Jerusalem. But when we left our home to return here to our work in the fields, morning meal had been prepared by a young maiden who told us she would be working with Mother; I noted that Lydia was not to be found. I had wanted to bid her farewell. Father was already

Yoshi of Bethlehem

out of the house at his work. Perhaps Lydia had gone into town for something.

Joseph and I set about moving the flocks when we returned, as we knew cold weather was coming. Our preference was to keep the lambs closer to our home when the coldest weather sets in. The hirelings had moved the flock in our absence, as we agreed upon before leaving. They were now in our furthest field, and we would graze our way back to the home pen. Since Jerusalem, Joseph and I had enjoyed many lively discussions in the evening around a warming fire about all the events we had experienced. By far, our most precious was being in the Temple crowd on the day that Zachariah had met with an angel in the Temple. This filled us with great hope for Israel and for ourselves. To think that the Messiah could show Himself soon was too much to understand. Joseph and I both knew of the prophecy that He would come from Bethlehem. But how? When? David had said a Root would spring up from Jesse. How exactly would that happen?

Weeks after our return to the fields, Joseph and I suffered a particularly demanding day. The flock had been grazing on fresh pasture as we moved closer to our home pen when a stranger and his entourage came up the path from

Jacob's land. No one typically uses that path so as they came with a noisy family of many children and several pack animals and a few sheep, our sheep became frightened. We tried to calm them, but our flock ran toward the southwest. The family's few sheep ran with ours as well. This was a rocky, hilly area and Joseph and I knew we were going to have trouble collecting them back. We noticed that a youth with the noisy family ran to retrieve his sheep. Joseph and I spent much effort running to catch up with the mixed group of sheep and in quieting them in order to walk them back to the area in which we wished to graze them.

The youth, a lad of perhaps 12 years in my estimation, fell behind but caught up with us as we walked back towards the field from whence we came.

"I apologize for this run, friends," the youth said. "I will take my animals and return to my family."

At that, he whistled loudly and called to his sheep. Six sheep came ambling out from among our flock and followed the young lad. Sheep do know their master's voice; he certainly commanded their attention.

Joseph and I held back a space to let the youth get his small flock ahead of us.

Yoshi of Bethlehem

We were both exhausted and hungry by the time we reached the field where the sheep had been quietly feeding just a short time ago. We were also curious as to the family who had disrupted us that day and caused such a fright in the flock, but we preferred not risking the mixing of our sheep due to threat of disease from his sheep. So, we chose to remain back and not speak any further with the lad who swiftly walked on ahead of us. He turned back only once to us to make sure he was taking the right turn in a forked area, but other than that, we did not speak.

The best we could muster for eating that night was a cake of bread we had made the day before and had planned to eat at morning meal but could not due to the running flocks. Even half of the dry, crusty bread made a great evening meal due to our extreme hunger! Joseph then lay down next to our fire for the night, and I sat looking at the heavens.

As I did each evening on the night watch, I prayed. Mostly I thanked our Great God for life and opportunity. I often prayed David's words. This night, among others, these words of his came to mind:

"Create in me a clean heart, O God, and renew a right spirit within me."

The next morning dawned clear. I had slept some that night as the flock did not stir at all; I knew they, too, were tired from the unexpected run during the day!

Joseph and I had built up the fire again and were working to prepare a couple of cakes with some figs. We looked up to find a large horse trotting towards us. It was definitely a Roman horse, as judged from its fancy saddle and blanket with multi-colored fringe.

As the beast moved closer, I wondered, "Now what with these Romans? It cannot be good news to have a Roman riding in our direction at this time of the morning."

My question was answered when I saw a familiar figure on the back of the horse, holding onto the Roman soldier. It was Lydia; dressed in beautiful attire and without her typical Jewish, face-covering headdress. In front of her rode "The Roman Friend." He was dressed in a Roman tunic and not in his standard uniform.

I was immediately irritated. I had prayed that the Lord create a right spirit in me just the night before, so I now had to accept that I could have a right spirit, even when disappointed by the sight which had stopped just in front of the gate to the pen.

Yoshi of Bethlehem

"Lydia," I said quizzically, "greetings to you…both; you are out and about early. You have news from Father or Mother?"

"Sister!" exclaimed Joseph. Why he always seemed to catch on that someone was present after the fact, I never could know! "How wonderful to have you visit us."

"Joseph and Yoshi, I wish to introduce you to Marcus Blandus Calvus. We come bearing various accounts. We also come with some foods."

And with that Marcus dismounted first and turned and helped Lydia from the horse. Lydia then produced a leather-looking bag that soon emptied of ever-coveted fruits, nuts, and dried meat. She even had some fresh cheese. My immediate thought was "where did she get the money for these items? Bethlehem's shops sell these at a great price!"

"Come, warm by the fire, and we can talk," I said.

Again "The Roman Friend" moved first and opened the temporary pen gate for Lydia. I felt somewhat awkward since I had not made any move to open it for her.

"Well, if he's earning my praise for being polite, it's working," I thought.

"Yoshi and Joseph, we must tell you our news first. We have married." Lydia certainly told us quickly and directly!

Well, my thought of praise for his being polite just flew out of my head as fast as a hawk swooping down for a field mouse!

"Married?!" both Joseph and I said this aloud almost too quickly at Lydia's statement.

"Yes. You probably saw upon return to Bethlehem that Mother had hired a servant girl. That was because I chose to return to Jerusalem. Uncle Roshan had quietly told me I would be welcome in his home should I choose to return and marry Marcus. Uncle told me that Marcus had already voiced his pledge for me to him, knowing that Father would not allow such a marriage. Thus, immediately upon our family's return and securing the servant girl, I left. I had not intended such a fast return, but there was a family which I could accompany leaving from Bethlehem the next day. It seemed best anyway."

I return in my recollections to the morning Joseph and I were coming back to the fields. I had wondered where Lydia was; I had not met the young servant girl before, and I felt it was quite sudden that she had come to our home to care for

Mother and the house. But, of course, Father said nothing. And now I realize Mother could not make her feelings or the situation known at that time.

Lydia continued, "I know that our union will be met with much resistance, but I hope that you two can accept us."

I assume this would have been a good time to say something, but I was blank.

Joseph spoke up, "Lydia, we will always claim you. And if you love Marcus, we will love him too."

I'm not really sure when Joseph had matured enough to say these words. And, although I was not happy about this Roman, I had to admit that Lydia looked happy, and Joseph's words seemed rather appropriate.

"Joseph, of course, is right, Lydia," I said looking directly at her. "We will learn to appreciate Marcus."

Lydia's demeanor seemed to perk up even further, and she stepped towards us to embrace each of us. That's the most physical I recall being with my sister. Joseph and I both gave a bow and nod to Marcus.

"Thank you for accepting us, Brothers," said Marcus. "There was no welcome in your father's home; Lydia has been deemed dead to Father and Mother."

I was not surprised by this statement. Jews just do not marry outside of the faith. It was religiously and civilly banned. And to marry a Roman! Well, that seems doubly blasphemous. Lydia did not appear daunted by the fact she was now not considered a family member by means of her marriage to a non-converted Roman.

Lydia and Marcus, now seated on our bedrolls to keep their fine apparel out of the dirt, had more to share. Lydia began, "There is another reason we came here to Bethlehem, Yoshi and Joseph."

"Yes," said Marcus, "we were excited to tell of our news of marriage, but we also have an official capacity here."

All at once, it struck me who this Roman was. He was the voice in the night speaking to Uncle Roshan that I had over-heard; he was also the Roman soldier with the reddish-purple plume on his helmet, who had come to the door of Uncle Ro-shan's shop demanding his tunic. I was trying to make sense of these memories, "What was there about them to recall?" But I could not sort them out even with this voice right in front of me.

"There is to be a census taken of all the Roman world," Marcus continued. "Everyone of age to be taxed is required to return to their city of origin. There will be a tax collected at that time. Your father will need to return to Jerusalem for that census since his family was first from that city. The census would also require that Yoshi, since he is of age, return there as well. However, I have arranged that only your father need return to Jerusalem. Lydia told me the hardship it would cause to again have hirelings here for your flock. You will not need to register in person; I have done that for you already, Yoshi. I actually did attempt to register your father as well, but his advanced age will require his presence and his tracing his lineage. Your registration was an easy matter."

"Thank you for doing that, Marcus." I had said his name yet again. It did not seem so bad! But maybe that feeling was also due to the gratitude I felt for his dealing with this. Knowing Father and Mother would need to return was enough to think about!

"Just yesterday an unknown family group had moved through the area," I mused aloud. "Then they were already aware of the census and going back to the town of the father's birth, I would suppose…"

"And Yoshi, I suspect Jacob already knows about the census and is permitting families to pass through his land and onto ours—for a fee, of course," Joseph added, "this seems how he operates; always taking advantage of someone."

"That is certainly feasible, Yoshi." Marcus continued, "The fact that your father alone is returning to Jerusalem is unusual as well; I knew from having met her already that your mother could not make another trip so soon. So, I also arranged for your mother not to be present. Your father could travel more easily and quickly without your mother."

"Lydia's husband is thoughtful," I pondered to myself, "I wonder if Father really understands how much he went out of his way to help our family with the census?"

Joseph asked more about the census for which Marcus was very knowledgeable. Maybe that was what he did as a soldier besides riding a horse? I was not certain. Perhaps time would tell more about this new person in our sister's life. But what a price she had paid to marry him!

Marcus and Lydia remained for a time; this gave me opportunity to study this man as we discussed the weather, shepherding, and Jerusalem. But Marcus did not talk about his activities as a soldier or the like. And I felt it improper to ask him outright. Joseph and I raided Lydia's food offerings and created a small feast for the four of us. The flock,

Yoshi of Bethlehem

thankfully, was content to graze in the temporary pen; I had intended to move them today, but one day longer here should not matter so much. I just knew we could not interrupt this visit with moving the flock.

Lydia told us about her new home in the Upper City in Jerusalem. It sounded lavish for a Jewish maiden from such a small town as Bethlehem, but we were pleased for her since she seemed so contented. The Romans did not always live with their families after marriage, and Marcus' family was in Rome, so it was an easy decision that he find a home for them. And Joseph and I concurred later that he must have a good salary to afford their fine clothes and to live in the Upper City.

Lydia's face did have a pained expression when I asked about Amariah and how he handled the news of their mar- riage. She simply explained that she had elected not to contact him since it could create interference for his religious teaching. She and Uncle Roshan had come to that con- clusion. She had returned to Jerusalem while Amariah was out. Uncle Roshan and Marcus quickly maneuvered her to a friend's property where she stayed until a civil marriage ceremony was conducted. There was no going back once she arrived in Jerusalem; the marriage was held four days later in a Roman law office after she was outfitted by Uncle Roshan with the proper apparel. Lydia did tell Joseph and me that having no family present, save for Uncle Roshan, was disappointing. All of these details were so different than what a Jewish maiden's betrothal and marriage would have been. I could not help wondering how disappointed Lydia was that only Uncle Roshan was present at the Roman wedding ceremony.

With the sun high and the afternoon rumination of the sheep, Marcus and Lydia determined that they must leave. They were to go back to an inn in Bethlehem that night, and they would return by morning light to Jerusalem. They both offered their welcome to us to visit in Jerusalem. I knew that would be next to impossible anytime in the foreseeable future, especially since we had just returned.

With another embrace of Lydia and nod to Marcus, they again mounted and went back towards Bethlehem. I was certainly surprised that they were welcomed in Bethlehem, but because of this new movement of people throughout Israel, I suspected the innkeeper was happy to lodge anyone—even a couple with an intermarriage of a local Jewish maiden and a Roman.

Joseph and I just looked at one another and began to quietly check the flock after Lydia and Marcus left. Neither of us seemed to have the words to express our current feelings. I was not even sure how I felt at the moment. Happiness for Lydia but sadness. Had Lydia decided to leave all her beliefs in God? How could she make the compromise to marry a pagan? What if she had never worn that progressive headdress that Uncle Roshan gave her, would Marcus have even taken notice of her when he stopped to help Mother? The marriage would always have a cloud over it, unless, of course, Marcus converted! But neither had hinted of any idea of that.

My most significant question of all, however, concerned the conversation between Uncle Roshan and this soldier. "What was the commodity they were discussing that night?"

"Baaaaa," the newest ram lamb was missing his mom. Back to my work—and quite gladly.

Chapter 13: Angels

It was two days past Lydia's visit when Father came to camp. It was a bright and warm day, considering we were already welcoming the cold season, and the flock was grazing away from the pen. I was trying to sleep while Joseph watched the flock when Father came. The night watch had been eventful with a howling wolf edging closer and closer but thankfully never attacking. Thus, Father's appearance over me as I rested by our lean-to was unexpected and caused me much confusion in my tired state.

"Oh, Father!" I exclaimed, trying to tuck time and person into place.

"Yes, Yoshi, sorry to wake you with a fright!"

"Blessings to you. It is good to see you. How is Mother?"

"She is fine, Son. I come with food supplies and an announcement about ..."

And here came Joseph, always last to anyone visiting! "Father, when did you arrive? I'm so glad to see you. Yoshi gets to be a bore; glad you are here." With this last sentiment, he plopped on the ground in front of Father who had also seated himself.

"Joseph, my son, you have sprouted taller since seeing you just weeks ago! Here are some foods, so, maybe we could have a cake and some figs," said Father. "I have brought you a quail that you will need to cook right away. He happened to be in my trap this morning as I was readying to come here."

"Sounds great to me." I quickly arose and took the items Father was emptying from his pockets. I also wanted to conceal the items Lydia and Marcus had brought two days before which were stored in our makeshift lean-to. That was the easy task; now to try to get Joseph to NOT talk about them having been here.

"Joseph, I was just about to tell Yoshi about the Romans' new nonsense."

Yoshi of Bethlehem

It was here that I began to worry about Joseph's maturity. Would he realize he should not talk about Lydia and Marcus?

"Yes?" I questioned quickly hoping to keep Joseph from speaking up, "What is happening?" And my mind already wandered to Lydia and Marcus telling us about the impending census.

The foods Father brought included already-baked cakes, so I simply pulled them from his various offerings along with some figs and distributed one of each to each of us. Meanwhile, I put another piece of wood on our small fire in order to place the quail across my cook bowl which was constructed of wooden branches. It was a relief to find that Father had even dressed the quail for us. I needed only to bake it on our fire.

Father spoke between small bites of his cake, "The Roman infidels have now decided they need to take a census. This is being done to know that everyone has been accounted for, so we can be taxed. They already have taxed us to our hurt, but obviously, we are not bleeding enough for them!"

For my Father, who was typically quiet and composed, this announcement about the taxes was made with an unusual amount of emotion that seemed stirred up in his being quite quickly!

"Yes," he continued, "they are requiring that heads of households return to their city of birth for this census. You know what that means, don't you?"

Joseph responded, "What does this mean?"

It was with this short response from Joseph that I could ascertain he was savvy to the fact he should not let Father know we already knew about this census from the visit of Lydia and Marcus.

"This census means they are counting everyone," said Father.

"But why are you so annoyed by the requirement about returning to your city of birth?" asked Joseph.

"Joseph, that means I will need to once again journey to Jerusalem. I was born there; my family lived there before the exile to Babylon. When we returned from the exile, that is the time that we were asked to move to this area. We were to take Bethlehem from its state of ruin and from being basically abandoned to rejuvenate and re-populate the area."

Yoshi of Bethlehem

"Yes, Joseph," I added, "don't you remember Father questioning where his family might have lived in Jerusalem when we were visiting? He thought that they had lived some-place near the Lower City's sheep market."

"Now that you mention that, I do remember you talking about that, Father."

"So now I must shoulder the expense and inconvenience of returning to Jerusalem. Had I known this some time ago, I would not have suggested our earlier visit to Jerusalem and would have used those funds for the trip for this annoying census!" Father's voice was picking up volume.

Father was standing at this point, "I just really dislike hav-ing to do what the Romans command!"

I was uncertain how to answer Father at this point, but I knew for sure that any mention of Lydia or Marcus could further heighten Father's fury!

"Oh, please, Joseph," I thought, "do not bring up their names!"

"The Romans need to return to their city of origin!" ex-claimed Father.

"Yoshi," said Joseph, "I think I smell the quail. Are you burning it? Father, he often burns any meat we happen to catch."

"Oh," I said as I barely touched my finger to the hot burn bowl situated over our small fire; I flipped the quail meat which was getting a bit scorched. "I think you exaggerate about my burning our meat!"

I felt some pride with Joseph at this point. He was defusing Father's fury by changing the subject, and he was avoiding the subject of Lydia and Marcus.

"Sons, I'm sorry. I told myself not to get upset over this and just to come and tell you that I will need to leave to take care of this. The Roman who came to inform me of the census also told me that since Mother is ill, I do not need to take her with me. That is a great blessing for her. I can go alone, but I would prefer that one of you go with me. You are both young and could make the journey on foot at a good pace."

"Sure," said Joseph. "Either of us would be glad to accompany you."

"Joseph, I believe it would serve me and the flock if that were you. I think Yoshi has more experience and should be the solitary shepherd for this time away. Are you agreeable to that, Yoshi?"

"Certainly, Father. However you wish to work this is fine. I can tend the flock."

"Well then Joseph, we will leave after Sabbath this week. Please move the sheep towards the home pen. That should help Yoshi considerably, and I don't think, unless I am wrong, that you've had them that close to the house for a time, so what grass is available at this time of year would be sufficient for them. I will also move some grains to the site to supplement."

"That should work out well, Father," I said. "You and Joseph should not feel too concerned about rushing. I know it is a tiring trip to Jerusalem on foot."

Father stayed a short time longer discussing his hope for increased pomegranate production for next year and talking about the chickens being less productive now that it was colder and the days were shorter. We spoke of Mother and her new servant girl.

At this point, I asked, "How is Lydia?"

Father responded, "Fine." Nothing else was said about her.

He talked about the increase of people around Bethlehem due to the census and their need for places to lodge.
He spoke of many things. But he never told us about Lydia
and Marcus stopping at home to announce their marriage; he
never told us about Marcus informing him about the census;
Father did not tell us that Marcus had arranged for both me
and Mother to not go to Jerusalem. In fact, he did not inform
me that I was actually supposed to go to register in the census.

It was apparent he was bent on not acknowledging Lydia
and her marriage to Marcus. And Joseph and I did not inform
him that we had our own rendezvous with Lydia and Marcus
and were aware of their marriage and of the census.

Joseph and I spent the next few days moving the sheep
some distance towards Bethlehem and the home pen. It was
odd, but the sheep seemed hesitant to move every day; it
seemed to unsettle them.

Equally unsettling to me was my constant question of
Lydia and her marriage to a Roman. My mind could not shut
off the many questions of their hasty wedding. Foremost
in my questioning was the significance of the conversation I
had overheard outside Uncle Roshan's shop the night Lydia

had told me about Marcus. The conversation between this husband of Lydia and Uncle Roshan was mystifying. As I re-thought the words spoken that night, it became more obvious to me that the conversation about the fine quality of the commodity and its benefit to Marcus regarded not textiles or animals, but people. And specifically, women. What was the meaning of this?

A couple days later and yet another family used the path between Jacob and us to get to Bethlehem, but they were not such a lively group as the first family, and our sheep did not seem too concerned about them. Joseph and I were quite happy the sheep did not get frightened! We also now knew why they were passing through.

The sheep were safely established in the home pen by Sabbath when Joseph and I had our short worship together and rested. Joseph actually spent more time with the sheep going into the night watch so I could get several extra hours of sleep. It was his parting gift to me, knowing I would find rest just a thought for the next days while he was gone.

A cloud-covered sun was just arriving, and the air was clear and crisp with a light dusting of snow falling when Joseph set out for home and his travel with Father to Jerusalem.

Father wanted to set out at morning light, but Joseph was a bit longer in leaving the sheep pen than he had planned. One of the rams had gotten out of the brush side of our enclosure during the night, so Joseph went to find him without waking me. He found him, Ramses, quickly enough, but he was not intent upon returning. Joseph finally encouraged his return with a wattle of thorns and branches tapping his backside in good nudges towards the sheepfold.

With all back into the pen and the wattle securing the opening Ramses had discovered, Joseph woke me and immediately set out.

But he set out with a mission from me: find out about Roman-Jewish intermarriages while in Jerusalem. Was there some reason this Roman soldier particularly wanted to marry Lydia? Was there some dividend from Herod, as Uncle Roshan had mentioned in the words he exchanged with Marcus?

My days without Joseph went well with all sheep on their best behavior. The night watches were always more intense with the increased lack of sleep as the days passed, but since we were moved into the home pen, I could relax some in the night watch. My first and second nights, sans Joseph, went splendidly.

Yoshi of Bethlehem

It was on my third night's watch that something truly amazing transpired. Something that even today, as I recount these events, I know was divine. Even many years removed, it is hard to put into words this joyous event. But now I know it was meant for not only me but for all the world.

It was well past the hour of the new day with a dark, dark sky full of twinkling stars. It was cold, and I had just sat down after I stoked my fire both for its warmth and for some security against the howling animals of the night. Suddenly there was movement in the heavens. At first, I thought this to be clouds moving in front of the stars in the vast expanse of the sky. But the "clouds" were swirling and twirling and grew ever closer. I watched, seemingly without blinking, as the swirling stopped before me. I was in awe as a shimmering Presence grew into the form of a host of Angelic Beings. I cannot truly adequately describe them except to say they seemed to be wearing raiment of the clearest but soft-looking and flowing material I had ever seen. They were radiating light so much that it was hard to look upon them for any length of time. However, my eyes were drawn to them; I looked at them and then looked away and then looked again and again.

Sharon Mullen

I had never witnessed anything so majestic; it made me a bit frightened, but I simply sat in wonder. I glanced at the flock which remained in a state of slumber.

I rose to my feet as the Beings came even closer. All I could think about was this being a holy moment, but I was unsure how to respond. They were so close I had to squint to look upon them—and there were many of these Beings. I was virtually surrounded by them! They were so bright it looked like the mid-day sun was lighting the sky!

I began to tremble with some fear, but mostly I trembled in awe. At this point, one of the Beings came to me in a melodic, soft voice: "Fear not, for I bring you good tidings of great joy. And this shall be to all people. For unto you is born this day in the City of David, a Savior who is Christ the Lord."

The Being went on in that soft tone, "And this will be a sign to you, you will find the Babe wrapped in swaddling clothes and lying in a manger."

I was dumb. All I could do was stand there and watch as this Being, joined by the others, began to cry/sing/talk (I'm not sure just what I would call it) in their soft, melodic, unified voices: "Glory to God in the highest and on earth, peace goodwill to all men."

Yoshi of Bethlehem

And then they left. Their light began to dissipate as they seemed to swirl and twirl higher and higher into the heavens. But somehow the night was still illuminated by their Presence.

The flock still slept. I stood and cried softly. This was such a momentous and spiritual encounter. My mind reflected on Zacharias' time in the Temple and the promise that he would have a son who was to prepare the way for the Lord. And now these angelic Beings were announcing His Birth, a Savior. The birth of The Messiah!

I am not sure how long I stood gazing into the heavens before the words of the single Angelic Being came to me in recall: I would find the baby wrapped in swaddling clothes in Bethlehem, the City of David. I must get to Bethlehem; this announcement was for the present, for me tonight!

I had never done this before, but I left my sheep sleeping in the pen and carefully and quietly closed the pen's gate.

I must go at once to Bethlehem.

It was then, as I reached for my staff and prepared to take leave, that I realized the angelic Presence was not gone. A ray of light shone, as if a lantern, to guide my steps on the path in the dark night. With the lighting from the Beings overhead, I quickly made my way toward the path that leads to my home and into Bethlehem.

What would I find? The Savior of the world born as a baby, as they stated? How could this be?

I passed my home on the path and went into the town square, as the light guided me. There I found several other shepherds whose accounts of the Beings in the heavens agreed with my account. We all knew we wanted to find our Savior. The Messiah. We Jews had waited many years for this blessed event. To be able to be part of this was overwhelming.

Chapter 14: Barn

There were seven of us shepherds intent on finding The
Messiah. As we gathered on the city square, the rays of light
each of us experienced coming in from our fields merged into
one bright light. I knew several of these men and had shared
stories of shepherding with them over the years during our
infrequent encounters. The Beings did not disappoint in our
quest to find Him; that bright light shone, and we merely followed its path again—away from the city square back to the
barn at my home!

    A typical home in Bethlehem consists of living quarters
on the one side with an animal shelter on the other side; the
home was often etched out of a hill or created by joining a
house to a cave opening. The house could be made with sun-
dried brick or made with a sort of thatch of dried mud with
straw reinforcement. It is during the cold months, as it now

was, that the family's few animals that were not kept in the fields were housed. My family was not wealthy, but we had built a comfortable, sun-dried mud house with attached barn and had acquired animals and some fowl which were housed in the barn due to the cold.

The merged, bright light directed us to my family's malodorous, drafty barn!

And it is there that we shepherds found what we sought.

A newborn baby...our Messiah!

God...in flesh.

He was there, wrapped in swaddling clothes and lying in our goats' manger just as the Angelic Beings had said. The God of the universe had stepped out of the history He had created to fulfill Scripture He had scripted. Next to Him, reclining on straw, was a young woman and slightly older man. Both wore the raiment of the poor. They seemed confused by our sudden presence.

Without a word, we shepherds walked forward and bowed at the manger. Seven well-worn men quietly filed in front of the manger, knelt, and worshiped our King. The King of the Jews, born of a woman as the Prophet Isaiah had foretold. My whole being was in awe and reverence!

Yoshi of Bethlehem

We had been there for a time when the man at the manger spoke in a low voice.

"Greetings fellow worshipers. You are witnesses to the greatest occurrence the world will ever know. Our Messiah has been born. We have waited four millennia for this blessed event. I would like to introduce us, I am Joseph, a carpenter from Nazareth. I came to Bethlehem due to the Roman census. And this is Mary, to whom I am betrothed. Mary was chosen by the Angel Gabriel to bring our Savior into the world. Gabriel first appeared to Mary and told her she had been chosen to bring Jeremiah's prophesy to pass, that He would be born to a virgin. When I found that Mary was with child, before we had finished our ceremonial year, I actually was going to divorce her privately. I had not been with her, yet she was with child. I could have easily used the Law to judge her because I did not understand this miracle. But Gabriel also appeared to me and told me to take Mary to wife and that she was still a virgin because the Spirit of God had come on her to father the Child within her. My Mary would be birthing the Savior! Our families were less than enthusiastic at our news, even cynical. It was both easy and very difficult to recognize Mary as worthy to bear our Lord. But then when her cousin Elisabeth, who is from Jerusalem—and married to a Priest named Zachariah—was also told she would be with child, the family's skepticism changed. You see, Elisabeth and Zachariah were older and …."

At this point, my understanding of these births meshed together. An understanding of epic proportions washed over me! I could pick up on Joseph's story. I had lived part of this story during my time in Jerusalem with Amariah! I had been there when Gabriel appeared to Zachariah in the Temple.

I interrupted with, "and Zachariah was told by the Angel Gabriel as well, while he was discharging his priestly duties, that he and Elisabeth, his wife who was beyond the age of childbearing, would have a son. Their babe's life would be used to foretell of The Messiah. In fact, Zachariah showed some disbelief with Gabriel and as a result was struck dumb, unable to speak. He was to be this way until the baby was born."

"Am I right, Joseph?"

By now I could see the surprise on Joseph and Mary's faces. "How could I know this?" I could read the question in their expressions.

Yoshi of Bethlehem

I explained my being in the Temple crowd on the day that Zachariah was in Temple and how that my brother was, in fact, one of his students. And I mentioned that they were actually in the stable that belonged to my family.

Mary and Joseph were crying. My story was further confirmation to them of the absolute destiny of their Child.

Joseph and Mary explained why they were in our barn with the Savior; there were so many people in town that there was no room in the inn. Mother heard of their plight at having no lodging, from her servant girl who is the innkeeper's daughter. While wary because Father was not home and there were so many strangers in town, Mother still offered that the couple could stay in the barn. Joseph explained that Mother thought they could rest a night or two in the barn, then a room at the inn might become available before the Child would be born. But God had other plans in coming. He came in the dark of night in a humble stable to two very unassuming parents.

One of the shepherds asked His Name. "Jesus; Emanuel, God is with us," was Mary's reply.

The Baby began to cry; Mary whispered that He was hungry. I was so proud to be a part of this time. The Baby needed attention. God, in human form, as a baby.

The angelic light began to dissipate. I knew I must return to my flock. The other shepherds sensed it was time to make their departures as well.

"May we see the redemption of Israel through this Holy Child. Blessings and long life wished to you and Mary and Baby Jesus," I said as I picked up my staff and started out into the night and to my flock.

But something caught my attention. Mary and Joseph must have traveled with a donkey to Bethlehem. And not just any donkey, there in the stable, contentedly munching on some hay, was Uncle Dathan's donkey. There could be no mistake from its markings. What an unbelievable turn of events that this "special" couple would end up with Uncle Dathan's donkey! I walked to him, patted his muzzle, and gazed intently at the "sun" etched in the fur between his eyes.

Mary had turned to the Child, and I motioned for Joseph.

"Joseph, did you purchase this donkey at a market in Jerusalem?" I asked.

Yoshi of Bethlehem

"Why, yes, I was in Jerusalem on business. But how would you know that?" Joseph asked with an incredulous look on his face.

I answered, "Because he had been stolen by the Romans from my father and me. When we were in Jerusalem on the visit when Zachariah had his encounter with Gabriel, we had gone to the main market. It was at this visit that we saw the donkey in a holding pen being led by a merchant. My father and I ran to the pen, but he had vanished by the time we could get through the crowd to the pen. We knew it to be this donkey, Joseph; no other donkey we have seen has his particular markings."

"You are right that the design on his head is unusual. Then I should return this beast to you to give him back to his rightful owner," said Joseph.

"No, Joseph, Father has already paid Uncle the price of the animal. He should belong to the family of our Messiah. You need him. I am sure my father would agree."

Mary asked for Joseph to come to her. That was my cue to finally take leave. The other shepherds were already filing out of the barn.

I saluted the other shepherds and walked back swiftly to my flock. Hours had passed since leaving them and finding the Savior of the world, but the sheep had slept through it all! I thanked God for watching over my sheep, but mostly I thanked Him for the tiny Babe lying in the goats' manger at my family barn, for this miracle.

So, God is flesh and with us. I would now resign myself to watching from a distance how things unfurl with both Zachariah and Elisabeth's son and Jesus. As I sat under the stars that night, with the light of the Angels having long ago vanished, I wished also that Amariah was here to see the Savior. The Messiah we had long awaited, born in our barn, but heralded by Angelic Beings whose Glory still amazes me every time I think of this wondrous event.

In another week, Father and Joseph returned from Jerusalem bringing news from Amariah that Zacharias and Elisabeth have had a son, as the Angel in the Temple foretold, and that he is named John. Amariah also sent word that this baby, John, was sent to be the forerunner of The Messiah. And Amariah reminded us that Scripture says that Messiah would be born in Bethlehem Ephrata. Our city. We should watch and wait for Him.

Yoshi of Bethlehem

Joseph shared the news from Amariah immediately upon his arrival back to the fields. I was anxious to speak to him of Jesus, but I knew he was excited to bear the tidings from Amariah, so I waited for him to talk first.

"Joseph, I, too, have news related to Elisabeth and Zachariah's son …" I finally said. And with that, I could finally tell someone about Jesus! I wanted to tell all of Israel about Him. Jesus, born in our goats' manger, wrapped in swaddling clothes and heralded by Angelic Beings. Joseph was in rapt attention as I shared my spiritual experiences of the past several days, and Joseph rejoiced with me as I told him about the Savior.

But Joseph had already heard about Jesus. Joseph let me finish telling every nuance of the night the Angelic Beings appeared to the time I returned to the sleeping flock after seeing and worshiping the Savior in our barn. Joseph then informed me that the town and the travelers in and out were all brimming with the news of this birth. People had come to Bethlehem for the census and were returning to their homes bearing the news. Others were passing through Bethlehem returning to their homes with the news. No matter their reason for traveling, anyone near Bethlehem was pulled into the drama surrounding His birth! Joseph said some who shared the news of His birth were absolutely astounded and went into Bethlehem immediately to see Him and to worship Him; others scoffed at the thought of The Messiah being born a baby—and to a young, virgin girl. They were obviously not learned in the Scripture.

Joseph reported that Uncle Roshan talked with him about Lydia and Marcus; he let Joseph know that the marriage was actually arranged. Lydia visited Joseph while Father was at the census site. Marcus was not present; in fact, he was on business in Bethlehem.

Father was appalled at the propaganda being spewed about becoming inclusive and accepting Roman rule and their customs and religion while he attended to his census duty. Roman lawyers walked around the census site encouraging intermarriage and intermixing of religions for the good of the nation.

Father talked with Joseph on their return trip to Bethlehem about Lydia and let Joseph know she had married a Roman. Father told Joseph it had been arranged—by Uncle Roshan. He indeed spoke of the propaganda that the Romans, and some Jewish leaders, too, were disseminating about these intermarriages being beneficial. Father spoke of two young ladies who went missing in Bethlehem. Could it be possible they were taken for such a disgusting practice?

That made my thoughts about Lydia and Marcus even dourer.

What I really wanted, however, was the chance to hear from Father himself about The Messiah. That opportunity was finally presented.

It had been a couple of months since Father had come to the fields with provisions for Joseph and me after his return from the census visit in Jerusalem. We were not in the home pen now, the sheep having grazed there sufficiently. The cold had started to turn to sun-filled warmer days, and we had moved the sheep further into our land for fresh pasture. But Father searched till he found us. I was so anxious to hear of Jesus. I longed for any news out of Bethlehem about this Babe. By now, Father had learned of Him; I was hopeful Father would speak of Jesus without being prompted.

Father spoke of his goats and new kids, his pomegranates and figs that were just beginning to take on new life in the warm weather and then informed us that Mother was feeling better and not coughing as she had a new interest.

"That is wonderful news about Mother being better. And what is that interest, Father?" asked Joseph.

"It is the Babe that was born. The One called Jesus. Yoshi, I understand you know about Him. The village is still enthralled with His presence. Jesus is now toddling about. Since His birth, Mother has filled her days with providing for the family and for the Baby, now a young Child. Mother spent little time in leaving The Messiah in our stable. She went from neighbor to neighbor both sharing the information of His arrival and seeking donations of food, clothing, furniture, and above all, a place for them to stay."

I was listening intently; Father called him The Messiah. I knew Him to be that; Joseph and Mother knew Him to be that. We were not sure that Father accepted Him as Savior.

Father continued, "Mother found that the Reubenite Family that lived just off the city square had journeyed to be with family near the Jordan and would not be returning to Bethlehem for some time. The brother-in-law permitted Mary, Joseph, and Jesus to move into their house. This whole matter of The Christ has made your Mother a new person. There is no coughing, no chills, no fevers. I don't know how this health has come upon her, but it is wonderful."

Yoshi of Bethlehem

"I am glad to know that she is so healthy, Father," I said.

But I could speak no further, as my ordinarily quiet Father continued.

"You know, Yoshi, that this family has Uncle Dathan's donkey. I spoke with Joseph of Nazareth, the father of Jesus, who told me you provided him the story of his being stolen and then sold in front of us in Jerusalem and gone before we could get to the holding pen. Yoshi, Joseph also told me that you had come to see the Child after being visited by Angels. I will not deny that Jesus' coming and events surrounding His coming have been miraculous. Even Mother's health is nothing less than a miracle." Father said with his voice cracking.

"And there is yet one more miraculous yet terrible event I must share. The young family moved into the Reubenite Family's home and had settled into life in Bethlehem. Joseph began to work with Benjamin the carpenter. The village continued to have visitors seeking to see this young Child, the Christ Child. One day a large entourage entered Bethlehem. They were from the East, from Babylon. There were five of them who were the obvious leaders; they were exquisitely dressed; your Uncle Roshan would have taken notes about their apparel! The leaders rode on fine camels. The beasts wore blankets of bright colors with elegantly adorned saddles and bits and bridles. These men from Babylon also had several slave assistants with them. It was apparent they were wealthy.

"They were astronomers and men of science. They were seeking Jesus. They had studied the solar system for years and knew that this Divine Intervention in the world would be arriving and when He would be arriving and that He would be born in Israel. In fact, they reported to us that they had followed a star which guided them to Israel. But they made one grave error seeking Him in that they went to Jerusalem, to Herod, seeking the Savior. They thought that as King, He would have been born in the palace of the king in Jerusalem. Of course, Herod's scholars knew of the Promise of the Messiah and could proffer that knowledge to him. So, Herod asked these wise men to come back to Jerusalem after they found Jesus and let him know where to find Him. Herod purportedly wanted to worship Him too.

"These men were warned by an Angel not to go back the same way they came and not to report to Herod where Jesus was born. The Angel informed these men that Herod had only jealousy and bad intent.

"The arrival of these men sealed my acceptance of The Messiah even further! They stayed in town for several days, expounding on the meaning of this Child according to astronological timing. They showed charts of the stars and tried to help those of us who wanted to listen to understand how to read the stars.

"Joseph, Yoshi, it was a beautiful time. I wished these men could stay for a long visit; they were so wise and very learned in Hebrew Scripture as well as astronomy. But they were warned to leave because Herod would be seeking The Child. In fact, it was about this time that the same Angel Gabriel who had told both Mary and Joseph that they were to birth the Savior, also came to Joseph and told him to flee to Egypt with Mary and the Child. Herod would be looking for Him shortly to kill him. And so, it is, Yoshi and Joseph, that the family left hurriedly with Jesus. Thankfully the men from the East brought expensive gifts to Jesus. With these, Joseph could purchase provisions for the arduous journey into Egypt. They were gone only four days when Roman soldiers came to town. They were seeking the Child. And then ..." my Father's voice dropped off, and he began to cry. He waved his hand to tell us to let him alone for a time.

Joseph and I exchanged quizzical glances; we had never seen Father so upset. What had happened?

He finally composed himself and spoke, "These Roman dogs took every male Bethlehemite child under the age of two and murdered them. Mikael, our servant girl, had her child ripped from her arms. He was taken outside her humble home and a sword thrust through his heart, while she watched in horror..."

Again Father cried, no, Father sobbed. Joseph and I both shifted closer but again he motioned us away and then he continued.

"Every young male baby was killed. There was weeping as I've never known it throughout the city. I am surprised that you did not hear it - even out here on these hills. The sorrow, the agony is still too much to think about. It was a bittersweet time, as we all know that The Messiah was spared. And how and when and where He delivers us from these Romans, I do not know, but I pray it is soon."

Father went on to tell us that he had sent for a scribe to come and write the happenings in Bethlehem so that he could send written news to Amariah. Father wanted to be sure Amariah was fully aware that The Messiah had come to earth, even though it was hard to understand how this Child would be used to defeat the Romans and bring Israel back to power.

With this visit, I could rest in the knowledge that Father now was as spiritually enlightened as I. In fact, he led Joseph and me in prayer for The Messiah's safety and soon return to Israel. He prayed for the families in Bethlehem who had children slaughtered by the Romans. He prayed with sincerity and with great ardor, something I had never experienced from him before.

The Messiah. How will this all end?

Chapter 15: Marriage

My hope of marriage to Asara reflected my great hope of Israel's future with the Messiah's arrival. With her I dreamed of a lifelong partner who would believe in me and offer me respect and comfort, and that she would willingly bear our following generation. I knew marriage to Asara was worth the wait, it was worth the past several years' work to save financially and worth the extra work with the flock to have them multiply and thrive to provide some livelihood for us. I was uncertain about how or when our Messiah would redeem Israel from Roman rule; I compared this wait to my wait for Asara and determined that this would be well worth the effort too. Waiting in hope for my love and for whom I know to be the One with All Love.

The betrothal year was upon us. I was able to leave the flock with Joseph in order to deliver the ketubah to Asara's family, as agreed upon in our marriage contract, just after the Feast of Unleavened Bread. Jehoram, her father, was pleased with the ram and ewe I had gifted; they were beautiful animals and should sire equally as lovely offspring. This gift was one that I could, of course, present, given my occupation; the gift was also to serve as the future livelihood of Asara's youngest brother. He would begin shepherding. He had been injured in a fire as a child and lost the use of one hand. Thus, Jehoram knew he could not follow in his trade of fine furniture making.

Asara's father, in turn, gifted us a beautiful bed he had made. It was complete with a soft mattress, much like Uncle Roshan had in his house. I knew very few families in all of Bethlehem had such an exquisitely made bed. The bed was to be placed in the small room in which Grandfather and Grandmother had lived in my parents' house. This was to be our home for the present. Since Amariah had joined the ministry and would live in Jerusalem, he would not be bringing a bride into the family home-place in Bethlehem. Asara and I would ultimately take over the family home at the passing of my parents.

Yoshi of Bethlehem

During this visit, I was able to speak with Asara at dinner with her family. It was truly the first time I would see her, not as a child, but as a woman. A soon-to-be bride. And she was striking. Since she was yet unmarried, her head was not covered. I was pleased to look at her long dark, wavy hair, her deep brown eyes, her short nose, her smooth mouth. God had formed a perfectly beautiful maiden whom I was glad to acknowledge. She answered my few awkward questions of the upcoming marriage with great poise. I wished later I had felt so dignified in what was my first real contact with her! This visit provided me the knowledge that Asara, too, had put faith into the One born in the manger in our barn.

Asara and her mother were gracefully and quickly providing a meal of venison porridge. I knew that my presence was of consequence to the family since they were providing meat in the meal. I felt humbled at this realization.

Jehoram, Asara's two brothers, and her grandfather were reclined with me to eat. Jehoram must have sensed my tentative start to conversation and opened the dinner with a discussion of shepherding and its importance locally and finished with a question directed at me.

"Yoshi, you have been in the fields for many years now garnering great experience. How many years has this been?"

"Uh, I was, I mean, I began tending sheep when I was about seven. My brother, Amariah, was still in the fields at that time but left for priestly duties shortly thereafter. I have remained now ten, almost eleven years. I believe that you know my younger brother, Joseph, is shepherding with me."

"Yes; I know from your father that Joseph has been working with you. You have done well with caring for your flock and for husbandry, it seems. The ram and ewe you have gifted us are both excellent animals."

Jehoram was a very gracious person, I sensed.

"Thank you for your kind words," I replied.

"Asara has been working with great enthusiasm with my wife to learn all her household duties well. It seems she has a great aptitude for working with the needle. Asara would you like to present Yoshi with your gift to him at this time?" asked Jehoram as Asara was passing a plate to her brother with the unusable arm.

"Father, I would like to wait until the meal has been served and completed, if it is acceptable," Asara responded, glancing at me with a wisp of red in her cheeks. Perhaps this was to have been a surprise for later. Either way, now or later, I was pleased with the surprise.

"Certainly, my dear," said Jehoram.

As Asara remained near the area in which we ate, I chose to take the opportunity to direct a comment at her.

"Asara, my Uncle Roshan, who has a tailor shop in Jerusalem, has agreed to provide a wedding garment for you. I am unsure if Mother has had the opportunity to speak of this with your father; no, I mean with you." I felt my tongue would not cooperate with me!

"Yes, Yoshi, in fact, Uncle Roshan came to our home for me to choose between two beautiful gowns. I think you know that his work matches nothing fashioned here in Bethlehem. I would love to sew like that, but I don't wish to be prideful," answered Asara.

"Yes, we are blessed by his generosity of this tunic," said Asara's mother from behind her. She was bringing a dish of unleavened bread. "Your uncle has now also seen articles of clothing she has sewn and has encouraged Asara to continue to use her talents. In fact, he felt that perhaps should Asara continue to show such great talent, he might share some of his load with her and would remunerate. He said he has other business in this area that could mean bringing work and picking up finished garments routinely."

"I find that highly unconventional," retorted Jehoram. "But I leave that decision to you, Yoshi. A woman working to be paid! He brings his Roman ideas to us in Bethlehem! Excuse me, please, Yoshi, I truly mean no offense to your uncle. But any ideas that the Romans push over on us, even through other people, I have a hard time agreeing with! And after the carnage here with our infants, I harbor great angst and great hatred of them. May God forgive me for my hatred."

"I am not offended by you. By the Romans, yes. But wait until Messiah delivers us!" I responded with great enthusiasm.

"So you put credence in the event of some months past, Yoshi? You believe that tiny baby is our Messiah?" asked Jehoram with a great deal of incredulity in his voice.

His voice made me know he was suspicious of Jesus and the claim of his authenticity. This put me at once in a great quandary. Do I respond with truth that I believe Jesus is Messiah or fold under the pressure of his non-belief and act as if I half-heartedly believe? After all, he is my future in-law!

Yoshi of Bethlehem

"I have every reason to believe that babe born here is The Messiah." I did not fold. In fact, Jehoram and his family permitted me to speak of my experience with Zachariah in Jerusalem, of my experience with the angels in the fields the night of Jesus' birth, and the experience of the visitors from the East providing for Mary, Joseph, and Jesus through their gifts, as they were warned to flee into Egypt with the baby. I told them about Uncle Dathan's donkey and its circuitous path to Jesus' family. I clearly stated that I felt these were not unanswerable coincidences, but signs that Jesus is Messiah.

When I finished, everyone just sat still. Two brothers asked to be excused and were given leave by Jehoram, but no one else spoke until Asara responded.

"Jesus, this child foretold by the Prophets of Old, He is Our Messiah."

I was surprised she was bold enough to make the statement, and yet I was so glad to hear Asara articulate what I hoped would be a common belief between us. Our Messiah has come. It would be a conversation I would share later only with Asara, but I wanted to discuss this belief and how it might affect our family as we waited for Him to save us from Roman rule to let Israel rise to great prominence again. Just knowing she felt the same towards Jesus was enough for now. Oh, how my heart danced at her confession of belief!

The talk for the remainder of dinner departed from the topic of The Messiah. I could have continued with that discussion with its questions and ruminations on the future of Israel, but it was apparent Asara's comment was Jehoram's end of discussion.

As I began preparing to leave to return to my work in the fields, Asara presented me with her handiwork that Jehoram had mentioned. It was a beautiful covering for the bed her father had made. Adorned with varying styles and colors of flowers, it was genuinely as lovely as anything I had seen in Jerusalem. I was quite proud of her work; I felt excited at her prospects for future work with the needle, considering she seemed excited by the blanket before me.

As I walked towards the fields, I felt overwhelmed that God would permit my marriage after the harvest to someone like Asara. Not only was she physically beautiful, but of more importance to me, she seemed to possess inner beauty. Her estimation of Jesus as Messiah was the crowning touch to my feeling of a joyous future with Asara.

Yoshi of Bethlehem

I got to the fields and reiterated the day to Joseph. At our evening prayer, I thanked God for so many blessings.

As Joseph prostrated himself in slumber and I milled about the sheep counting and checking, I could do nothing more than look heavenward and praise God for the hope of the future ... with Asara ... but more importantly, with Messiah!

Chapter 16: Sorrow

It has been some years since hiring a scribe for dictation.
Many events have taken place during this time, which brings
me to my writing now. As my hero, David, once said, "I once
was young, but now am old..." I pick up dictating again where
my life left off—some 30 years prior—to share the miraculous events that I have been a witness to that have changed
Israel and all the world's religious and political history. That
my family has been involved in these happenings is of great
consequence to me.

At the end of my last writing, Jesus the Messiah had
been born; Amariah continued in Jerusalem studying the
priesthood; Joseph was tending sheep with me; Lydia had
married a Roman soldier; I was betrothed to Asara.

Indeed, Asara and I were wed after the harvest. It was a
lovely event marred only by Father's refusal to permit Lydia

and Marcus to attend. Father had indicated to me at that time that their marriage was arranged by Uncle Roshan; it was for political and financial gain for Marcus. Father was indignant towards Uncle Roshan when he appeared bringing Ketab, his assistant, to the wedding. He had also brought Amariah, which lent some air of acceptance to the presence of Uncle Roshan and Ketab. And Father remained civil towards Uncle Roshan during our week-long festivities. I did not know until later, from Joseph, that Father's ire towards Uncle Roshan was so remarkable.

Apparently, the conversation I had overheard with Uncle Roshan and Marcus when the family was visiting Jerusalem when I was but a youth, just a few weeks before Marcus' marriage to Lydia, involved the sale of young Jewish maidens. That was the commodity that they were discussing that I could not totally figure out at that time.

Herod was offering both salary and rank increases to any Roman soldier marrying a Jewess. This was his vain attempt at conciliation among the Romans and Jews and his idle effort at the subjugation of Jews by intermarriage. He knew that intermarriage was forbidden for a Jew, but he also knew it was a means of rallying morale and oftentimes actual civic, religious and financial support for Rome.

For Uncle Roshan's part in Herod's scheme, he felt he was helping young, poor maidens and their families by matching them with suitable Roman soldiers who could provide well for them. Although his intentions were somewhat noble, they were displaced. Father felt Uncle Roshan's pride in being aligned with Romans caused him to pursue this horrible practice. Uncle Roshan paid Jewish families living in abject poverty to relinquish their daughters, and in turn, the Roman soldier marrying her would be paid handsomely by Herod. Uncle Roshan evidently was honestly mixed up in this confused affair only because he felt all parties involved benefited. He did not stop to consider the loveless, unequally religiously aligned marriages he was arranging.

But in all of this confused mess in which Uncle Roshan had participated, Lydia and Marcus were evidently quite happy in their arranged marriage. For Marcus, this started out as a means of political improvement and a great increase in rank and salary; for Lydia, however, she genuinely cared for Marcus immediately upon meeting him. She articulated that to me. She had no knowledge of Marcus's gains by marriage until they were both enjoying a blissful relationship. Forgiveness and grace are two important accessories in any relationship! Marcus had callously agreed to this arranged marriage for his own gains, but this Roman soldier, who could be brutal at times, softened and gained a loving partner. There is more to their story that I will dictate later.

After my arranged marriage to Asara, I returned to the fields with Joseph. I was quite content knowing I would return to my new wife every few months. Asara proved a great worker with the needle as Uncle Roshan began to provide work for her to undertake for his shop. Uncle or Ketab would bring items for tailoring, and they would return with pieces Asara had so beautifully rendered. It was a rather financially beneficial arrangement for our family.

But that arrangement proved to be a clouded looking glass. What I thought was a business arrangement was apparently something more nefarious. Joseph was the one to find out…

I was to return to the field after three days and two nights at home. I had particularly wanted to be present when Uncle Roshan's assistant, Ketab, came to exchange tailoring work with Asara. Joseph and I had moved the sheep in the

pen closest to home since I was to leave all sheep in his care
for that time; he would be night and day watch, and that pen
closest to home was large enough and secure enough to provide for the sheep for these days.

Ketab had come with garments for Asara to sew; she
had given him those that were completed since his last trip to
Bethlehem. With that accomplished, he thanked Asara and
provided her the remuneration Uncle Roshan had previously
suggested. He loaded his beast with the freshly sewn garments and headed towards Jerusalem, as we bid him farewell.
I thought it odd and even remarked to him my surprise that
he would set out on the return journey with night coming on
before too long. Out of safety, most travelers were hesitant,
even afraid to travel at night. He responded that he would
be stopping for the night somewhere along the way. My mind
was questioning, "Where?"

Unbeknownst to us, however, Ketab was only making
the appearance of returning to Jerusalem. As the story
would unfold later, after he had gone only a short distance
to get out of sight of our property, he turned his beast back
through a neighbor's field and towards our path that connected to Jacob's land to the south. In the midst of this cir-

cuitous route, he had also gained the presence of a mounted Roman soldier who had been waiting for Ketab.

It was at that point that Joseph gets intertwined in the story. As the afternoon heat was diminishing and the sun began to lower, Joseph was away from the pen gate checking on the sheep. It was evident later that he was with a ewe about to lamb. He must have been heading toward the well to fetch water before dark to return to the ewe and must have been unseen by Ketab and the Roman. As best as can be suggested by events, soon Ketab and the Roman were joined by Jacob who had traveled up through our land by beast. But he was not alone; a young Jewish maiden was mounted before him. She was the daughter of a poor shepherd to the south, I would later find. They must have stopped close to where Joseph was, but he had concealed himself purposely.

And Joseph must have witnessed the transfer of the maiden to the Roman. This was one of Uncle Roshan's "arranged marriages." But from the later account of the maiden, she was not a willing participant in this arrangement. She did not wish to go with the Roman. She began to cry and wail and attempted to flee. Ketab and Jacob became angry and yelled for her to stop struggling. A lash was soon extricated from

Yoshi of Bethlehem

Jacob's tunic. The Roman dismounted and began to speak to her while running his hands over her young body. She continued to struggle for release; Jacob lifted the lash and began to strike her.

Meanwhile, the sheep were becoming alarmed. Joseph was even more alarmed at the mistreatment of the maiden. He had to have known it would be at the expense of keeping the sheep calm, but he tore from his hiding spot and ran into the fray of three men whipping and fighting one defenseless woman. Joseph grabbed the lash which Jacob had used fiercely against the maiden. She was lying in a heap on the path trying to protect herself from the leather strap. According to the maiden, Joseph ran to Jacob and grabbed the lash, held on tight and prevented Jacob from striking the maiden again. He asked Jacob to put it away. Jacob angrily refused only to wrest it away from Joseph and turn it on him.

While Joseph was being beaten with the leather strap and attempting to grab it again from Jacob, the Roman had seized the girl and tried to mount his horse with her. Her continued struggles made him slip and land flat on his back on the hard ground. But he still had his churlish Roman hands on the maiden.

By now the sheep must have been even more alarmed at the sound of their shepherd's raised voice; they began to move frantically towards the pen gate which they had entered and exited many times. And, again according to the young girl, Joseph yelled wildly, evidently deliberately causing the sheep to run. And they ran in the direction of the path where their shepherd's voice had been heard.

Ketab had already physically detached himself from the frenzy and had moved a distance away on the path toward our home.

The sheep running was the maiden's salvation from the Roman. The Roman saw them coming before Joseph and Jacob who were now both on the ground and fighting by hand. The Roman had just enough time to mount and out-gallop the stampeding sheep. And the fine gentleman he was, he had released the maiden leaving her on the ground with no thought for her safety.

Jacob was mortally trampled.

The maiden, however, had stretched herself in line with a fallen tree and miraculously was not wounded by the sheep.

By now, I had heard the commotion from outside our house and was running to the field. As I reached the crest of a small hill just before the sheep pen, Ketab was racing past on foot, pulling his beast as fast as he could. I did not feel I could stop to ask him about the commotion but obviously wondered what his part in this was. He was supposed to be gone. I could hear the sheep bleating and running. And as I ran toward a now-empty pen, I saw two men laying on the path. A young girl was bent over the body of one of them that I knew to be Joseph.

"Joseph, Joseph, my brother. What has happened? Joseph…" my voice trailed off on a wail of agony. "Oh, Joseph." I cried as I lifted his shoulders and put his head in my lap; his eyes were closed. His head was bleeding and torn from the hooves of the sheep. Blood oozed from his mouth, an eye socket, a gash on his forehead, and from an ear and pooled quickly on the ground. I tried to stop the blood with my sleeve, but the flow was stronger than my feeble endeavors. I rocked and cried.

"Oh, Joseph, Joseph. Please God, help us…" I begged.

I began my favorite Psalm, "The Lord is my Shepherd…"

I felt Joseph slightly stir. "Could there be hope for life?" I thought.

I looked in Joseph's contorted and mauled face. He opened only the one uninjured eye.

"Yoshi, I could not help Cleopatra to birth. I am sorry..." he said in a whisper.

And he was gone. His soul was released to God while I held him and wept. And his last words were those of a caring, true shepherd; words of worry over one of the ewes.

The unfamiliar maiden, too, lifted her voice and wept. I had momentarily forgotten her.

And there lay Jacob, the supplanting neighbor. His soul, too, was released for judgment from an Almighty and Righteous Judge.

By this time Father had also come to the field. He found his youngest son already gone to Sheol. We carried his limp and still bleeding body home.

The next days and nights were a sorrowful time. Joseph was laid out in Father and Mother's home immediately. The young maiden who had been torn from her family proved a God-send. We found that her name was Johanna, meaning "God is gracious." Johanna personally assisted the local ladies who cleaned up Joseph's body, anointed it, and covered him with a shroud—a new tunic Asara had tailored for him not

many years before served as this burial shroud. These chari-
table ladies made sure to place an appropriate covering over
his face for others not to have to look at the horror of his
wounds.

What Bethlehem lacked as a small and poor village it did
not lack in respect for life and death and family issues. It
took very little time for the village to gain knowledge of Joseph's death. They arrived in the late evening and night darkness for the funeral. His body could not be left too long out
of the ground. Mourners arrived, and pipers came. Friends
came; Asara's father arrived with a hastily made but beautiful burial box. The villagers came and stayed with Father
and Mother, joining them in their sorrow and listening as they
spoke of their youngest son.

Joseph was carried to his earthly resting place by other shepherds who had come in the middle of the night out
of respect for Joseph's occupation. They had prepared the
final resting place. These same shepherds had also rounded
up the flock, mended the pen gate, and secured the sheep
inside again. Posted with the sheep were the same two itiner-
ant shepherds who had been hired when we took our leave to

Jerusalem many years before. These shepherds would end up staying on permanently.

My consolation in his death was in knowing Joseph's goodness and in discovering he had died attempting to save the young maiden from the Roman infidel. As the days passed, in my mind and in the telling to Asara, I re-lived many nights when Joseph and I sat in the fields with our sheep, amazed by the grandeur of the heavens and the God who made it all. We had times of fun together as younger shep-herds frolicking with the sheep; we had our share of concern with the care of our flock and their safety; we had times of refreshing in the Presence of God as we quoted Scripture and prayed. We had shared many things as brothers. We had shared many things as friends. First Amariah had left; now Joseph had left me. This great sense of loss was lessened with the knowledge that Asara was with me, supporting me, caring for me.

Uncle Roshan and Amariah arrived early afternoon the next day after Joseph was interred; they arrived on mounts which explained the speed at which they could travel. But how did they learn of his death so quickly? Ketab. And he was with them as well. And how would Father react to Uncle

Yoshi of Bethlehem

Roshan's presence considering he had probably orchestrated the sale of the Jewish maiden, Johanna, to the Roman soldier who caused Joseph's death. And the presence of Ketab here? That could be Father's final insult.

I had been resting and reflecting outside alone when I saw them.

"Amariah, Uncle Roshan," I exclaimed, not caring to include Ketab in my greeting, "how did you find out about Joseph?"

"Yoshi," Amariah shouted as he dismounted and ran to me. As we embraced, he told me, "I am so sorry about Joseph. I wish I had known him better. We came as soon as the runner...as soon as Ketab informed us."

"Yes," said Uncle Roshan also dismounting, "I, too, am very sorry to hear of his death."

I was not certain how to accept Uncle Roshan. How could I forgive him for his part in Joseph's demise? And why would he bring Ketab?

"Yoshi, I wish to tell you that I had not arranged this maiden's sale," Uncle Roshan said hurriedly. "I had no knowledge of any of this."

As if he had been called, Father came upon the four of us. It left me no real time to sort out my own feelings about Uncle Roshan and Ketab. Instead, a sense of what might happen with Father now prevailed.

"Roshan, you have some grit to show up at my home at a time like this. As if the death of my youngest son is not enough, you bring your assistant here. The very man whom you used to cause death to Joseph!" Father's voice was raised, and his face was red. But I sensed his redness was more of a reflection of grief than of anger.

"Please Joel, let me explain," Uncle Roshan said, and he continued with, "There is more to this than you know which I must divulge."

"No," said Ketab, "I must explain."

"Ketab," Uncle Roshan interjected, "let me…"

"No, sir, please." Ketab continued. "The sale of the young maiden to the Roman was not Roshan's idea. It was mine. As with Gehazi of old who was greedy and wanted the riches Naaman had offered Elisha upon his healing of leprosy…"

I was immediately dumbfounded that Ketab would know this story. How could a pagan from another country, as I thought of him, know of Elisha? Perhaps Ketab was Syrian? And maybe that story was told differently by his people?

"…I, too, was greedy. Roshan had re-considered his sales of maidens to Romans. He told me he wanted no more to do with them and had even informed the Captain of the Guard for whom he had previously made such arrangements."

"Ketab, no," said Uncle Roshan. He seemed to wish to protect Ketab from his admissions.

"Yes, I should continue," said Ketab. Uncle Roshan deferred to him with his head slightly hung.

"This last arrangement had been previously made. It had already been arranged that the sale would transpire when I was here delivering and picking up garments from Asara. But Roshan had canceled this sale. I went behind him and told the Captain I would coordinate the delivery of the maiden to the Roman. I meant no harm; but I was, as Gehazi, greedy. I knew I could take the denarii and that Roshan would never know. Or so I thought."

Ketab suddenly looked as if he could collapse. "I alone am responsible for this horrible outcome. I will bear the punishment you exact, Joel."

Restitution in Jewish law for death was death.

Quickly Uncle Roshan spoke up. "There is more to this that I must tell now. I know from Jewish Law it will be of no consequence, but I wish to let it be known. Ketab is not only my faithful assistant, but he is my son. When we found we were barren, Gershona and I used the story of Abraham and Sarah and decided to take matters into our own hands. Ketab is the offspring of a Roman servant girl."

Father had chosen to sit upon the ground by now, and the rest of us followed. I am not sure if he was so overcome his legs gave out, or if he was so exhausted from grief and the events of the past hours.

Uncle Roshan continued, "It was never a good time to tell the family. And since we lived so far from you, we decided to raise him as my assistant. He is indeed a capable assistant, but he has also proved to be a fine son, until this indiscretion now."

With the last comment Uncle Roshan turned to Ketab. "I am grieved by your greed, but I know that I am to be blamed for that. Perhaps my interest in always making another denarius has caused such a breach in good reasoning for you, Ketab. I am sorry for that. I failed you."

Yoshi of Bethlehem

Uncle Roshan then turned to Father. "Joel, I do not know how, but if it takes my own life, I wish to make restitution for the death of Joseph." Uncle Roshan, not one in my estimation for emotion, was now crying hard and laid his head upon the knees of Father as a sign of humble acceptance of what was to come.

Father sat for a time with tears rolling down his cheeks. Amariah was crying. Ketab sat, softly weeping and moving back and forth. I was so overcome with grief and the truths that had just been put forth that I could only sit there looking from one face to the next. The mourners could be heard from inside Father and Mother's house. Mother was no doubt being comforted by their presence. I did not know what comfort could be found outside here in the midst of these relatives and these revelations.

"Yea, though I walk through the valley of the shadow of death, I will fear no evil," intoned Amariah. He continued to quote Psalms, and then he prayed: "God, please give us direction in this time of grief and need for restitution..."

Father, Uncle Roshan, and Cousin Ketab worked through the elders of the village for restitution. Father was relied upon heavily to set the restitution requirements with the elders

201

backing away from influencing the outcome. In the end, it was determined that Cousin Ketab would continue to pay for the maiden to work for Mother. He also paid her family handsomely in order to lift them from their financial plight. Both Uncle and Cousin openly and remorsefully pledged their cessation of involvement in arranged Jewish/Roman marriages. They were also to make an atoning sacrifice at Temple. Uncle Roshan had felt such guilt through the years due to the birth of Ketab through a Roman that he never became involved in religious activities. In fact, Amariah's training was part of his personal atonement for Ketab. The arrangement was made in private: Father would not bring them before the gate to be judged.

Chapter 17: Nicodemus

Amariah remained in Bethlehem for a time after Joseph's death. Uncle Roshan and Ketab returned to Jerusalem after making restitution as prescribed by Father. Uncle Roshan and Cousin (such a strange new way to think of Ketab) were to return for Amariah well before the time of Purim for which Amariah was to participate at Temple. It was determined that Asara would continue her sewing for Uncle; Uncle and Cousin were to be welcomed back into our homes without residual ill will towards them.

Amariah had been following Jesus' ministry carefully from Jerusalem. On a previous visit, Amariah told me many things about Jesus' family that he had learned through priestly channels. And they evidently knew a lot; the family was being carefully monitored by the Jewish leaders given that Joseph and Mary and many others were claiming Him as Messiah. I knew through Amariah that the family had moved back from Egypt to Nazareth after the death of cruel Herod. No true Jew mourned this ruler's loss.

Joseph and Mary returned to their families in Nazareth both to skepticism and to many who believed that the child with whom they returned was God in the flesh. As with the learned men from the East who had come to Bethlehem when he was a young child, visitors continued to bring Him gifts and worshiped openly in His presence.

The presents brought by the more affluent provided for the many indigents who traveled to Nazareth to see Jesus; Mary even helped the poorer visitors leave with a warm belly thanks to the gifts brought to Jesus. Many came. They wanted to see their Savior. However, Mary and Joseph were careful in providing only a glimpse of Him. He was a child growing up in meager circumstances, learning His Hebrew and studying the Law, working with his father in the carpenter trade, running, and playing. He did what the other Jewish male children of his age were doing, except that He was God in the flesh. Some travelers were bewildered by the fact that His life was so routine.

Yoshi of Bethlehem

"What really was the likelihood of this being Messiah?" they questioned openly at times with Mary and Joseph and the priests.

"How was this child to exact a toll on Rome that many desperately wanted and had waited for so long? How could this child save them from physical and spiritual oppression?"

Amariah said these were questions he also had, but they did not make Jesus any less God in the flesh.

Jesus' parents had other children, and when Jesus was about 12 years old, He went to Jerusalem to the Temple with his siblings and parents and extended family. As with my family when I was about this age, the trip no doubt held special meaning both in a natural sense and in a spiritual one to Jesus. I could totally understand the story Amariah told me about this visit. I personally remembered the feeling of not wanting to leave the Temple grounds when I was there because the atmosphere was so full of the awe of God. Jesus was so versed in Scripture, more than any Jewish boy who was taught at home, that He stayed at Temple and expounded Scripture with them for a couple of days—with Amariah there as a witness of His great knowledge.

"Yoshi," Amariah had told me, and I remember this well, "no one but God could have known Scripture and could have known the details of our Patriarchs and the miracles in their lives which all lead to the founding of our great theocratic nation, Israel. He knew intricacies and events that happened hundreds of years before that we priests continue to research but could not find in our Holy Scrolls."

Amariah shared that this visit had firmly established his belief of Jesus as Messiah to him. God alone could know all that Jesus expounded and taught with the priests while he was at Temple. But Amariah said he had to be very careful about this belief. Many of the other priests, including the High Priest, were unmoved in their estimation of His being another fraud. They were not interested in trouble with the Romans over this proclaimed Messiah. And they did not want another sect of followers to rise up and cause problems. There were those who had called themselves saviors: Theudus, Judas the Galilean, Simon, others; each had raised an insurrection against Rome only to be brutally squelched in their endeavors.

It was during this visit to the Temple that Amariah and his priest friend, Phillip, had even provided a sleeping spot

Yoshi of Bethlehem

for the young lad, Jesus, in a Temple storage area. His family had gone to their encampment for the night without Him. Amariah said he and Phillip wanted to stay and talk more with Jesus, but they could tell He was exhausted, so after producing a bit of bedding for him and a small lamp, Amariah and Phillip left Jesus to rest. They were surprised the family had left Him. Jesus seemed unfazed by their absence.

When Amariah and Phillip arrived the next morning for their prayer time, Jesus was already awake, before the sun was risen, and walking around the Temple grounds in prayer. Amariah and Phillip had brought him bread and cheese and fresh juice which Amariah said Jesus willingly accepted!

I also recall well how Amariah said that it was an awesome wonder to see Messiah, as a young lad, both wise beyond anyone's imagination as He was the God of all things, but also tired and hungry as His earthly body required sleep and food. What a holy paradox!

The third day He was settling in again with Teachers of the Law. Many had heard from other priests that Jesus' teachings were phenomenal, to say the least, and priests and students of the Law had come from other areas of Jerusalem and beyond to hear Him. In fact, The School of Law in which

Amariah taught was moved to Temple that day so all students could be there to hear Jesus answer questions from the Jewish leaders and impart His wisdom. Gamaliel prompted the first question, "Jesus, yesterday you left off telling us about Enoch, Moses, and Elijah. You told us that these men were so righteous that they were caught away into heaven...."

However, the meeting had only begun when Jesus' family arrived at Temple.

"Jesus, Jesus," a loud voice rang out, cutting off Gamaliel in mid-question.

Jesus stood up amidst the scholars. "Father!" He said, seemingly surprised.

"Jesus, my son, where have you been? Your mother and I have been looking for you all over Jerusalem!!" Joseph, Jesus' father, cried with a loud voice oblivious to the fact that scores of men were listening to the dialog between the two.

"Father, you know I must always be about my Father's business. I have been here teaching..."

By now they were embracing with Jesus no longer looking like an authoritative figure but again like the young lad he was.

"We must go," said Joseph. "Your mother waits in the outer court."

Yoshi of Bethlehem

"Surely you don't mean just to remove Jesus now?" asked Gamaliel with some disbelief in his voice. "We have assembled to hear Him speak again. He has wisdom beyond His years."

Amariah said that Joseph explained that they had gone back toward Nazareth a distance when they realized Jesus was not among the family caravan. Jesus had traveled to Jerusalem with a large entourage of family and Joseph and Mary had thought Jesus was with his younger brothers and cousins who had run ahead to fish and bring back their catch for the family to eat that night. The brothers and cousins returned bearing a great number of fish, but Jesus was not among the cousins!

Thus, Mary and Joseph returned to Jerusalem as quickly as possible and were relieved to find Jesus at Temple and to know that He had been provided for by the priests. Amariah and Phillip decided it was not in their best interest to divulge that they had been involved in supplying Jesus' provisions.

But Amariah reported that while Mary and Joseph had been worried about Him and fretting about where He was, Jesus had simply answered that He was doing "His Father's business." Amariah and Phillip again realized Jesus was referencing His eternal being as "Father." Amariah told me that he and Phillip spent many hours pondering and studying that one comment!

Amariah and Phillip continued to follow Jesus in clandestine fashion. They knew the Chief Priest and rulers were not happy about His presence; these priests could not answer just who He was, but they were stubborn in their refusal to believe that Jesus was God, our Messiah.

On a visit after the death of our brother Joseph, Amariah reported how Jesus, now as a man of about thirty years, had gone out to the Jordan River where initially His Cousin John, Zachariah and Elizabeth's son, was immersing people in the muddy Jordan as a sign of their asking for their sins to be removed. Some years before, Naaman had humbled himself to be washed in this very river to be cleansed of his leprosy; was there a parallel to this Syrian commander's finally obeying Elijah's command to dip in these waters and being cleansed and this dipping of John's followers for being cleansed? John did not require the people to make sacrifice at the Temple for the removal of their sins; instead, they were told to be immersed in the water unto repentance. Jesus Himself was dipped by John!

"What does this mean for us?" I asked Amariah.

Yoshi of Bethlehem

"I believe, Brother, it means that Jesus has come with changes to be made to our religious thinking and practices."

The first night of this visit, Amariah shared much about Jesus' changes with Asara and me and Father and Mother. But after that first night, others from the village came to hear Amariah tell of the many wonders he knew of Jesus. It was sensational, but many believed that Jesus was Messiah and wanted to know all that Amariah had experienced or heard as both a priest with access to information and as someone living in the area from which Jesus was teaching and preaching.

Amariah and his friend, Phillip, were ardent followers of Jesus, but they still remained cautious of many of the Jewish leaders. At every opportunity, Amariah and Phillip, as well as select Jewish leaders, were traveling to wherever Jesus was to hear Him and see the wonders He was performing. In fact, Amariah and Phillip were reprimanded by other members of the teaching faculty and Jewish leaders for being seen among those following Jesus. Amariah had been reminded that he was being considered for a place on the Council, the Sanhedrin, as a young member, but that offer could be withdrawn if he were found with Jesus.

But Amariah continued his quest to learn more about Jesus. Amariah confessed to me his belief that Jesus is Messiah; there was no question that He was come according to the Scripture and had, and would, fulfill the prophesies made about Him.

Amariah's friend, Phillip, had a brother named Saul. This brother had attended The School of the Law before Phillip and had studied under Gamaliel as well. But this brother was otherwise minded about Jesus to the point that he told Phillip not to keep listening to Him or seeking to find Him. Saul warned Phillip and told him to tell Amariah as well, that this Jesus was a farce, a deceiver, and that He had come to destroy the Jewish way of life and turn Israel upside down religiously, socially, and politically, and to cause trouble with the Romans. Saul and Phillip's Jewish family were originally from Tarsus in Cilicia but came to Israel when Saul was young; this made them dual citizens of Rome and Israel. Phillip, according to Amariah, always questioned Saul's loyalties to the priesthood. He wondered if it was a ruse for his more politically Rome-minded dealings with the Jews in Israel.

"In fact," Amariah had told me, "Saul was present at the Temple just before Passover when Jesus came and found dis-

honest money changers and people buying and selling their
sacrificial animals." Amariah retold that Jesus was disturbed
by this; He asked them to leave the Temple grounds, but
those who were selling were belligerent and defiant and would
not acquiesce to Jesus' demands. Jesus then turned over
the tables of these merchants, scattering their animals being
sold for sacrifice, and took a cord to the money changers
and made them leave. Saul also overheard Jesus tell a group
that He indeed did have power. And Jesus said that not only
could He cleanse the Temple in this manner but also told them
that if the Temple were destroyed, He could raise it up again
in three days!

Saul was incensed by Jesus' claims of authority and power and at His audacity at driving out those who were using the
Temple as a mercantile. Amariah's friend, Phillip, believed that
this day was the turning point in Saul's overwhelming vehe-
mence against Jesus. And his fervor against those believing
in Jesus as Messiah was heightened. Saul was determined
that Phillip and Amariah both reject Him.

This visit was such an enlightening time with Amariah.
My years of questions about Jesus were being answered by
Amariah's revelation of Jesus being God in flesh. Amariah

stressed that Jesus taught many times that His Kingdom was not of this earth and that we should do good towards one another. He spoke of a heavenly kingdom to be attained; it was evident Jesus did not plan to establish an earthly kingdom, which is certainly what most Jews thought was His purpose. How would He deliver them if Israel was not set free from Rome?

Amariah told us that many were being healed by Jesus. How could He not be God? Blind men had their sight restored; young children were made healthy and were playing again; the deaf were hearing; the lame were walking. Amariah said that there was no end to the healings and deliverances from evil spirits that Jesus had performed. Amariah had heard from another priest that in his area, Cana of Galilee, Jesus had attended a wedding where the family ran out of wine. Jesus had water pots brought in and changed the water in them into a fine drinking beverage. And it was reported to be better wine than that being initially served!

But the skeptics continued questioning the miracles; why did He not choose to heal everyone who came to Him? Jesus' own earthly father, Joseph, had died. Why did He not heal

Yoshi of Bethlehem

him? Why not provide financial blessings for everyone? Why not free Israel from Roman suppression?

Amariah told Asara and me privately about an experience one of his mentors named Nicodemus had with Jesus. Nicodemus was a great Jewish teacher. He was of the sect of the Pharisees and a ruler among the Jews. He was pious and very revered for his knowledge of the Law. Amariah felt he had gained much of his scriptural knowledge from this teacher. Nicodemus had recounted His visit with Jesus to Amariah but was not intending to share this with others at The School of Law. Nicodemus was intrigued by Jesus. He wanted to know for himself if He was truly Messiah. So much of what Nicodemus was hearing was astonishing and hard to believe, and Nicodemus knew, if these things were true, no one but God could accomplish them. He already felt no one but God could teach as Jesus could teach.

So Nicodemus came to Jesus under cover of darkness. He was very eager to talk with Him, to understand Jesus and to come to terms with Jesus' claims to be Messiah. With great candor, Nicodemus talked with Jesus, and He answered Nicodemus' questions. Specifically, Jesus talked of a new birth.

Sharon Mullen

"Jesus," Nicodemus asked, "how can I be born again? Do I enter my mother's womb again?"

"No," He responded. "This is not a natural birth. You must be born of the water and the Spirit."

Amariah recounted that Jesus told Nicodemus that the water birth was through the act of being dipped in water. This immersion of people in water was a form of spiritual birth. And Jesus also explained the need for baptism with the Spirit. John the Baptist had alluded to this when he spoke of Messiah: "He shall baptize you with the Holy Ghost." Nicodemus and Jesus evidently talked for quite some time that night. As the sky began to lighten with the dawning of a new day, Nicodemus told Amariah his spirit was lightening as he clearly saw Jesus, the baby born in Bethlehem and raised in Nazareth, as the Savior of the world. Jesus told Nicodemus that He was the Light. People who do evil do not like Light or their deeds will be known. So, Nicodemus now knew with certainty that he loved the Light, believed in the Light, and would follow that Light.

Chapter 18: Trouble

Asara and I had not seen Amariah for several months. In fact, sadly, his last visit was due to the death of Mother. After the birth of Jesus, Mother had lived almost thirty-two more years. And the reason for her longer life? The only thing Mother and we as a family can attribute this to is Jesus. Before His coming, her coughing fits were such that we never knew if she would regain her breath to continue in life. After His birth, Mother was miraculously healed; healed the very night He was born. In fact, several other people in Bethlehem reported having no more long-term health problems after that night's events.

Mother's faith in the Baby named Jesus was incredible. In fact, it was her faith in Jesus as Messiah God the Healer, the Provider, and the ever-Caring Lord that helped Asara and me as we waited many years for the gift of children to be added to our marriage.

Asara and I felt blessed but melancholic when our oldest son, Thomas, went to the fields as a shepherd. It was difficult in a natural sense to release him, but we knew unequivocally that Messiah God was with him in birth and would be with him throughout life. This brought our family to six children at home. With Thomas now in the field, the dynamics of our home shifted, but it was still full of activity and loud. Due to his age and faltering steps, I took up the care and rearing of Father's feathered flocks and took up his gardening of pomegranates and figs. Asara continued to sew for Uncle Roshan and Cousin Ketab. In the past when they came from Jerusalem to bring clothing to sew or pick up items, they would bring news of Amariah. Now, often they did not have such news as he had moved into a room at The School of Law as part of a promotion in Jewish leaders' ranks. His friend, Phillip, also had been promoted and was living in another area in the school.

More than news of Amariah, Asara and I groaned for news of Jesus and what was taking place in Israel. Through

Yoshi of Bethlehem

members of the community, at times we learned of where He was and how the crowds reacted.

It was nearing the Feast of Passover. Several had come from areas around Bethlehem choosing our best rams for sacrifice at this most sacred time. Many of them brought news that Rome was becoming increasingly uneasy with Jesus and his followers, also known as disciples. Jesus' ministry was up-ending Israel, but in a spiritual way, not a political one which some Jews could not understand. Why was He not freeing us from our political oppression? Rome remained in control in Is-rael, but it seems, as told us, that the Romans were very wary of Jesus because He had amassed such a following.

Asara and I had not heretofore been to Jerusalem to-gether. Passover would prove an exceptional time for a family visit and religious sacrifice which we had determined some months before; we had also agreed that we could financially afford the trip. We had sent word to Amariah through Uncle Roshan and Cousin that we would be there near Passover. Our family would lodge, as I did many years ago, with Uncle and Cousin. Father, due to his age, would remain in Bethle-hem. Thomas would come in from the fields to accompany the family as well. In fact, Thomas was about my age when I made my first visit to Jerusalem. This would prove such a great family experience.

Thomas, as Joseph and I had done some years before, chose the ram to take for sacrifice. Thomas was tender-hearted towards the flock, just as Joseph and I had been. Even with our two hired shepherds, Thomas was always the one to stay up nights with the birth of new lambs and the one to walk mile after mile in search of a lost animal. Sheep just could not remember directions! On this trip, Thomas kept careful watch over the animal on our journey. He made sure he was well-watered and fed and kept very clean. I would glance to find him running his hand through the ram's fur. As with me at his age, he was already reluctant to have to eventually release the ram for sacrifice. But he knew the importance of this religious gesture.

And so, we packed up our seven children and one ram and began our trek to Jerusalem. We had journeyed for some distance without any problems. However, Asara tripped on the path while playing with our children at a rest break. As she fell forward, her right ankle twisted awkwardly. She was in immediate pain.

"Ayyy, Yoshi," cried Asara. "I have injured my ankle!"

Yoshi of Bethlehem

"Let me help you up," I said as I reached down to her.

"Oh, I cannot walk on this ankle, Yoshi. What will we do?" asked Asara.

"Perhaps we should have brought a beast after all, Asara," I said. "I really thought it best with the crowds that will be in Jerusalem not to have a beast. Even now, there are more on this path heading toward Jerusalem than there was yesterday."

Meanwhile, Thomas picked up a reasonably thick branch and broke off the small branches from it.

"Father, Mother, can we not use this to secure the foot?" Thomas asked.

I already knew Thomas was a smart lad, this just cemented that feeling.

"Yes, that's perfect," I said.

With Asara's already-swelling leg now tied to the branch with strips of cloth from my robe interior, Thomas and I could share her weight between us. This just meant that our last part of the journey to Jerusalem would be walked very slowly. It also meant our next son, Samuel, was in charge of the ram. Even pilloried, the ram's leading was difficult for an unskilled "shepherd," as he was now calling his six-year-old self.

We finally arrived at Uncle Roshan's as the last lights in the day sky were making way for the dark night sky. Tomorrow was the Passover. I had hoped to arrive earlier to make preparations for the Passover feast.

Amariah was waiting when we got there. Uncle and Cousin were off on one of their many fabric collecting journeys, according to Amariah. Marcus and Lydia had been waiting for us until it was dark enough that they needed to leave.

After embraces all around and the exchange of small chatter, it was apparent Asara was spent.

"We might find a physician tomorrow, Asara, if you would like that," Amariah said with some tenderness, as we carried her to the main guest sleeping room and laid her on the thick bed that I had not seen on my last visit. This would have been the room of Mother and Lydia on our past visit.

"I should be fine after I rest," Asara said with some trembling to her voice. Evidently, she was enduring great pain. "I do not wish anything to eat, Yoshi. I will rest now."

Thankfully, Uncle's servant girl had prepared us a now-cold meal of porridge and bread. But we thanked God for this provision and for His care for us on our trip. Amariah helped me feed and put the children to sleep; as much as they

were excited to be in a new setting, they, too, were quite weary. Amariah wanted to place them all in the room with Asara.
She did not stir as we placed mats and coverings on the floor
for the children, and each quickly slipped off into slumber.

"Yoshi, I am thankful that you are here. I have so much to
tell you about Jesus. And while telling you of The Messiah, I
will tell you of Lydia and Marcus. You will want to hear all."

"Jesus," I said, "Amariah, I want to hear everything you
know of Jesus, please."

Amariah told of the many wonderful works of Jesus. He
spoke of his teaching and how that throngs of people met
Him wherever He went. Some, he knew, came only for the miracles; they did not understand Him, they were in awe of Him,
yet they could not accept Him as Messiah.

Amariah revealed even more about the Jewish leaders
and their hatred of Jesus. How could they hate someone
they did not know personally or spiritually? But they sought
any occasion to try to trick Jesus into being ungodly; they
tried to trip Him up on Scripture and prophesy in front of
those He was teaching to lessen His impact. Nothing they did
mattered. He was God; He knew their thoughts and motives.
He overcame all their challenges.

Just last week, Amariah informed me the Council met. He and Phillip, as members-in-waiting, were called to this meeting. When they arrived, they were surprised to see Saul present. They were unaware that he was working within the Sanhedrin; he neither spoke to them during the meeting nor after. Phillip and Amariah were amazed at the purport of the meeting: Jesus must be stopped. He was too powerful; too many people believed in Him as Messiah. This Jewish Council just wanted things to go back to their sense of normalcy with the Romans in rule and the Sanhedrin in their rightful place religiously ruling the Jews and assuaging any issues that surfaced with Rome.

"I don't know how much further the Council will move against Jesus," Amariah said with some air of concern. "They are jealous of Him; they are less concerned about the many prophecies His coming has fulfilled than what fits with their idea of how comfortable they had become before Jesus was born. The Messiah is quite simply being rejected by those who should have accepted Him the most. The Passover is to-morrow," Amariah continued, "and I am worried there may be some attempt to discount Jesus' ministry. I know He will come to celebrate the Passover with His disciples."

Yoshi of Bethlehem

"Yoshi, I must tell you that I made a great determination after that Council meeting. I renounced my member-in-standing with the Sanhedrin. I am no longer welcome to teach at The School of Law. I have been relieved of all of my Temple duties, and I am not to attend any of the Council's religious meetings."

"Amariah!" I said with surprise. "What does this mean?" I heard what he just told me but could not fathom the depth of his sacrifice for Jesus.

"It means, Brother, that I have no standing within the Jewish religious leadership. I let it be known that I was a believer in Jesus as Messiah. As such, I could not accept their stance that He was just a religious fanatic with a large following who needed to be dealt with, maybe killed. Phillip also made his belief in The Messiah known, as did one other young member of the Council. We were all three immediately ushered out from the Sanhedrin chambers. In fact, Yoshi, Saul, Phillip's brother, was one of those who made certain we physically left the Council immediately."

"This must have been hard to do, Amariah. You have studied and worked so hard for your position. And I can only guess that this has caused a rift between Phillip and his brother, Saul."

"No, Yoshi," he said, "this was one of the easiest decisions of my life. I will follow the Christ till my last day on earth. I have been, as has Phillip, with Him on many occasions to see His work, to hear His teaching. In fact, Phillip and I were both baptized by Jesus. Phillip's brother has disowned him; Saul won't even speak to him. But Phillip, too, believes in Jesus to the point of losing all of his family. At first, we secretly traveled with Jesus and his followers. We have seen Him heal scores of people. There were so many people healed by Jesus in the campaigns when I was present that I could never recount them, Yoshi. Jesus said many of these people could not or would not accept spiritual healing unless they had physical healing first. Many of those healed then did accept Him as Messiah; others accepted only their physical healing and went away. Who knows whether their unbelief caused their illnesses to return? Phillip and I called this 'convenient faith.'"

"Amariah, I will always be thankful to Jesus for healing Mother. She would never have had so many years with us if

Yoshi of Bethlehem

His coming in our barn had not ushered in the healing Mother needed."

"I agree, Yoshi." He paused. "And Yoshi, there were many people who were full of evil spirits that Jesus cleansed. I could tell you of occurrence after occurrence of supernatural abilities I have seen in Jesus. Phillip was present when He fed a multitude with but a few loaves and fishes. Truly the sad part of this is, despite all of these miraculous and unexplainable events, our Jewish leaders have chosen to reject Him. Our Messiah. It is sad, Yoshi. I feel that they want Him eliminated. Here's where I want to interject my story of Marcus and Lydia, Yoshi. It is interesting. I had gone out to Bethphage to listen to Jesus teach. Phillip could not come this day. He was teaching at School, and we were still trying to not bring attention to the fact that we were so interested in Jesus. So, he could not leave. I had taught my morning classes and then walked to Bethphage. I was careful not to tell anyone, except Phillip, where I was going. Yoshi, on my way there, a group of Roman soldiers on horses passed me going into Bethphage. I thought one of the soldiers was Marcus, but I did not call to him. Again, I was trying to be discrete as I attended Jesus' teaching this day. I got to the square in Bethphage where normally someone would know where Jesus was teaching and point the way. But there was only an unruly bunch of Roman soldiers there. This was the same group that had passed me. And this time, I knew it was Marcus I had seen pass, because he saw me and turned quickly away from me. He then mounted, called to the others in Latin and they quickly left. I waited a few minutes, and several townspeople came out from the shadows, as they were fearful of the soldiers. They told me these soldiers had come and disrupted the meeting with Jesus and had Him and His disciples leave the area."

"Really, Amariah?" I queried, "And Marcus was one of those soldiers?"

"Yes. But that's not the end of this, Yoshi. Some weeks in the future both Phillip and I had gone to hear Jesus teach, and a group of Roman soldiers showed up. Marcus was again among them. But this time, Jesus was already teaching. In fact, He had evidently healed a young girl just before we arrived. The crowd was still talking about it, and we heard it from one of Jesus' disciples. His name was James. Phillip and I stayed close to James. We wanted to savor every connection to Jesus we could. We were just being seated with James

Yoshi of Bethlehem

when this band of Roman soldiers and their horses came into the outskirts of the crowd. I immediately saw Marcus, and he saw me but did not turn away, as he had previously done. The Romans did not ride into the crowd as I assumed they had done in Bethphage from what the villagers told me. They stopped, tethered their horses and then sat on the ground on the perimeter of the crowd. They were not there to disrupt; they were listening as intently as I was to Jesus speak. Yoshi, I so wanted to stay with James, but as soon as Jesus' message was completed, and many were pushing forward to have Jesus touch them, I got up and went to Marcus. This time, he acted happy to see me. I certainly was thrilled to see him, especially in light of the fact he appeared to be there for the same reason as I: to know more of Jesus."

"Amariah, you have made my heart leap. Tell me, Brother, did Marcus make any indication that he truly believes in Jesus as The Messiah."

"He did not go that far. It seems he had been instructed by his Roman superiors, who had been instructed by Jewish leaders—think Sanhedrin—to interrupt Jesus' meetings. Marcus said he and his men started doing that. Marcus and his men on several occasions found out where Jesus was to teach, and one of those occasions was Bethphage when I arrived late. They took their horses and broke up the crowd to make them scatter. But while doing this, a couple of his men, and then Marcus himself, began to feel somewhat guilty about their actions. So, they discussed this among themselves, and the next time they found Jesus teaching, they listened. And the next time, they listened. Finally, some of the soldiers, including Marcus, looked forward to finding Jesus so they could listen. Yoshi, Marcus said he had never heard anyone speak with such authority, and he's been around a lot of Roman authorities."

"So, does Marcus profess belief in The Christ?" I asked.

"Not in the way you and I do. I think Marcus is trying to understand just who Jesus truly is," Amariah responded. "But I am praying for him to understand. I am so excited for him and Lydia. In fact, I have now been to their home on several occasions to help Marcus and Lydia with their struggling faith. It is exciting, Yoshi. But it does put Marcus in a precarious position as a soldier. I hope we may see them while you are here in Jerusalem."

Amariah then went on to explain that tomorrow at the Passover Feast, we must be watchful, careful. He felt the

Yoshi of Bethlehem

Jews were going to work against Jesus at this very important feast. They wanted to make an example of Him to the Jews and to the Romans, which was certain from the last Council meeting he had attended. How? He was not sure.

"I had you place the children in your sleeping room and not in the spare sleeping room because I am now occupying that room, Yoshi. I had to move all my belongings here to Uncle Roshan's. The Council has cleared any references to my teaching at the School and at Temple. They have done the same with Phillip and the other School member who left with us."

"Amariah, I am proud to be your brother. I know you have made this determination with much prayer and wisdom."

"Yes, much prayer, Yoshi," said Amariah. "Both Phillip and I feel a peace about Jesus and being His followers. But now, Brother, I think we should sleep. We will need to arise early tomorrow to prepare for the Passover. And we should attempt to get to Temple early due to the throngs that have come for Passover. Let us pray for Jesus and what tomorrow brings," Amariah instructed. And with that, he led us in a beautiful prayer for this earthly God-man, Jesus. We were praying to God about Jesus, His physical representation here in Israel! How could the Jewish rulers not understand Who He is? There were so many signs and Scriptures fulfilled with Jesus.

When prayer ended, I left Amariah after an embrace and joined Asara and the children. I quietly slipped onto a sleeping mat, but my mind was as overstuffed with thoughts of Jesus and Marcus and Lydia and Jesus and Amariah and Passover tomorrow as this mat was overstuffed with soft material.

"Amariah is no longer considered a Teacher of the Law by those in power in Jerusalem..." I thought, and I finally drifted off to this huge resolution.

The roosters of Jerusalem were welcoming morning as I awoke. Somehow, they seemed louder in the city! Thankfully no one else in the room was stirring, and I made haste to go in search of Amariah. He had already been in prayer. I only wished I had not slept through his prayer time and could have joined him.

The servant girl had prepared a morning meal yesterday as well as the Passover meal. She was Jewess and had been trained for such feasts. I felt a sense of disappointment for Asara, I knew she had been looking forward to preparing the Passover meal, but her injury had lengthened our trip such that we did not arrive in Jerusalem as planned for her to cook. Thankfully there had been someone ready for the family's arrival and need to eat.

I joined Amariah as he sat reclining.

"Yoshi," said Amariah, "we must speak about our plans for the day. I have been thinking..."

No sooner had Amariah began to share his thoughts for the day when my family quickly joined Amariah and me on the roof where the morning meal was being served. The quiet morning erupted into family prattle as the children came and were greeted and hugged by Uncle Amariah. The noise did abate some as each was given some of the fruited bread previously prepared. Asara walked the few steps to the roof, leaning on Thomas. We three adults discussed the day. Asara would not go to Temple. Her leg was too painful. Due to the crowds, it was decided that the younger children would remain with her at Uncle Roshan's. They seemed pleased with this decision as they had just discovered a kitten on the roof in the sitting area.

"Thomas," I said, "after you have eaten, please prepare yourself and the ram for the walk to Temple. Uncle Amariah and I will find you in a short while."

Amariah and I excused ourselves and hastily left and went into Uncle Roshan's adjoining shop to talk. I remembered my last encounter in this shop! It was a secret chat with Lydia about Marcus. Lydia and Marcus. I was hopeful they were moving spiritually toward belief in Jesus as Messiah.

"Yoshi," Amariah started immediately, "there has been a trial overnight for Jesus. James, His brother, sent a runner to me very early this morning to bring the news of all that occurred. This is a total travesty! It is not lawful for the Sanhedrin to meet at night. The Council had Him brought before them on charges of subverting the Roman rule as He states that Rome has no authority over Him, as He is God. The Council found Him guilty. They created these charges so that they could transfer Him to the Romans for answering the charges against Rome. I knew the Council was set against Him."

"Oh, no. What of Jesus? What will happen?" I asked.

"It may mean long imprisonment or even death. However, the Romans do not believe in compassion for crimes against Rome; their sense of justice for someone supposedly inciting the masses against Rome is swift and cruel. This is exactly what the Sanhedrin was seeking, any reason for Jesus to be dealt with by the Romans. One of His own disciples, Judas Iscariot, led an armed crowd to Christ, with orders for seizure from the Chief Priests and elders. I cannot understand that act of disloyalty, Yoshi." He paused before continuing. "Jesus was taken to Pontius Pilate. He is the Roman Governor. His crime presented to Pilate was that Jesus claims to be 'King of the Jews,' thus destabilizing Roman rule. If found guilty, this crime's punishment is certain death. Yoshi, I think we need to prepare to leave right away. I suggest we do not take the ram now. I know the importance of a sacrifice at this time espe-cially, but I wish to go directly to Pilate's Hall. We must find out what is happening with Jesus. We can return for the ram if all goes well."

Chapter 19: King

Amariah, Thomas, and I quickly prepared to leave. I had talked quietly with Asara about the events concerning Jesus. She, too, worried about the outcome for Jesus, but she also begged that we be cautious. Who would know what the Romans might do—or even the Jewish religious leaders! In fact, in the end, Asara asked Thomas to stay with her, in part to help her get around, but I also knew she had some concern for his wellbeing. I could not argue against either consideration; he somewhat reluctantly stayed at the house. However, he, too, wanted to play with the new-found kitten and tend to his ram.

We walked out of Uncle's house to the increased noise that we already heard within the baked walls of Uncle's home. I was rather startled at the number of people who milled around in the streets; no doubt many of them intended to take part at the Temple observance of Passover. Since Amariah knew his way through Jerusalem's back alleys, we were slowed by crowds for only a short time. We then walked briskly toward the unknown. What was going to happen today to Jesus? This question was the impetus for haste. It was still too crowded to be able to walk abreast with Amariah and too loud for me to be able to discuss this burning question.

Amariah lead me through passages that were normally tight, but with crowds larger than I had seen on my first trip to this city, the areas were almost impassable. We waited for breaks in groups to be able to move or to politely push past others. We walked quite a distance and then the street opened up wider and then wider yet again. Still filled with people and animals and voices and dust, we continued our quick pace over the dirt, then rock-littered, and then brick-lined streets.

I felt a sense of foreboding as we started on the brick-lined streets, as if my present world was going to encounter a shift in its equilibrium today. These streets signaled more of a refined and deliberate construction. They were not the streets of the everyday Jew; no, the Romans had laid these streets and probably with Jewish slaves doing the work. Father's dislike of the Romans had permeated my soul. I could not get around that fact. And for some reason, partly due to Amariah's words last night, our course to find Jesus and understand what mere men were doing with the King of kings made me sense that the Roman involvement would be substantial, possibly tragic.

The edifices on these brick-lined streets were also very refined; I had seen such before on my previous trip to Jerusalem when going to the Upper City and to The School of Law. These were obviously the homes and meeting places of the wealthy, those in rule, and those in commerce. It was no surprise that the place we sought, where Pilate the Roman governor lived, would be in the best area of the city. As we neared, Amariah pointed out a great white building ahead which was our intended stop. It looked magnificent from a distance, but I neared to find its grandeur was breath-taking; even more spectacular than those buildings of the wealthy I had seen on my first visit to Jerusalem. It was a massive fortress with thick and highly decorative walls and large openings with grand stairs that lead into an edifice where marble seemed to be the chief building material.

There was a din coming from this fortress, and we encountered another crowd here. It was apparent that many in Jerusalem knew of the Council's arrest of Jesus. As I surveyed the crowd, I saw from their apparel a mix of the poor in their rough and mended robes to those in finely tailored colorful robes. The poor and rich, financially and spiritually, mingled over the consequences of Jesus' arrest.

We stopped where there was a very wide opening in the fortress walls and a great platform-type area. This place, I later learned, was called "The Pavement." Here Pilate sat and conversed with the Jews and discussed matters of crimes and punishment. It was also known as "Pilate's Judgment Seat."

This crowd was being held from "The Pavement" by a large contingency of Roman guards. It was readily apparent that the crowd was divided in their beliefs in Jesus. Some stood quietly while others wildly yelled for "the great savior," "the farce," "the deceiver," or threw other unseemly words at Jesus.

Amariah and I looked ahead at the platform area which was empty. Where was Jesus? What was happening?

Those questions were quickly answered as Amariah found a previous priest "friend" in the crowd, or really the "friend" found Amariah. It was apparent how he felt about Jesus.

"Good day, Gesham. Blessings to you. You also came for news of Jesus here at the Judgment Seat?"

"Amariah," the man sneered. "I have much news of this rebel. He has been charged during the night by the Sanhedrin with the crime of subverting the rule of Rome. He is now in the hands of the Romans. He will get what he is deserving, Amariah. You were foolish to believe in this fool."

So the crowd gathered here obviously also knew that Jesus had been charged with this "crime," I thought.

Before further conversation, Amariah and I saw a figure step out from the back of the platform area. Amariah had told me earlier over the clamor of the crowd that Pilate would come from an area behind the platform. The figure wore a blue flowing gown adorned with golden-colored objects on the neck and down the arms. It was an exquisite gown; one that I could envision Uncle Roshan tailoring. I deduced right away that this expensively gowned man was he. Pilate walked forward on the platform to a railing and waited.

Gesham took this moment of interruption—with our sights on Pilate—to quickly move away from us. But I noted that he moved from person to person and spoke to them with the same sneer on his face that he had when he greeted Amariah.

"Yoshi," said Amariah, "there is Saul, Phillip's brother." He pointed at a man who had left a doorway in the area from which Pilate had just walked.

"That he is part of the Council's rejection of Jesus, I am certain. What part he has with Pilate in this, I am not sure. But his meeting with the pagans is not a good sign. Why would a Jew choose to be seen leaving that area?" I knew this last question from Amariah was posed for his own reflection and not to be answered.

So that is Phillip's brother, Saul, I mused. I studied him carefully as he exited the platform area. He was taller than Phillip but equally as handsome.

Soldiers moved forward on the platform before Pilate and pointed with their long spears for quiet. They then began to shout at the crowd for quiet, first in Aramaic and then in Latin. The crowd was restless and pushed and shoved from behind us. Amariah and I locked arms to remain together.

Yoshi of Bethlehem

With what seemed the best quiet the soldiers could muster, Pilate moved between the guards.

"Citizens," he yelled in Aramaic above the still-noisy crowd. "I am come to speak of the man, Jesus."

With His name mentioned, a roar went up from the crowd. I could not ascertain if it was of support or rejection, however.

Pilate continued his discourse. "I have received from the Sanhedrin this man who has been accused of being King of the Jews. As He has called Himself King, he is accused of subverting Roman rule."

Again, the crowd responded with a resounding roar. I could make out many yelling, "No!" while others were chanting, "Jesus, Jesus."

Pilate lifted his hands and regained a modicum of quiet.

"I sent Jesus to Herod Antipas, since Jesus is from Galilee, and it is Herod Antipas who rules that region. Herod Antipas found no real reason for judgment against Jesus and has returned Him to me. I find no fault in this man for judgment either."

The crowd again pressed forward; many yelled unholy blasphemies. Amariah and I fought hard to remain together, even with locked arms.

I glanced around the crowd and saw faces full of anger and ugliness. Yet, I also saw faces that seemed to reflect sadness and questioning. While I surveyed the crowd, I saw Saul with Gesham; they moved together in the crowd and spoke hurriedly to individuals and to groups of people.

I turned back to the platform as Pilate motioned to his guards. I watched as a door in the distance opened. Many guards with their swords drawn filed out, and then they brought Jesus.

Jesus, my Messiah. My Lord. My King. This One in whom I believe even though I had only seen Him as a baby and heard of Him and His wonderful works through the last thirty plus years. My Redeemer.

I wanted to bow in His Presence, but the crowd became even more unruly with the sight of Jesus. Curses were yelled at Jesus with more fervor than ever. I could not believe what I heard directed at Him.

Jesus was brought forward by the guards, and it was quickly apparent that He had suffered great physical abuse.

244

Yoshi of Bethlehem

His face was gashed, and His eyes, His lips, and His cheeks were puffed and swollen. Guards were holding Him upright.

I glanced at Amariah whose tears flowed. I felt utter sadness and helplessness from the appearance of Jesus and from the certainty that there had been cruel treatment thrust upon Him.

All at once, the crowd became still. No one pushed or yelled curses. It was as if something holy had been sensed. And it was just that, the holiness of my Lord was palpable. His human nature was evident with the beating He had suffered, but holiness radiated from His very Presence. I believe everyone in the crowd sensed the magnitude of His holiness and were in awe of Jesus. I was overcome with emotion; my Messiah, my "God with me" stood on Pilate's platform.

Pilate seemed to understand the crowd's immediate respect for Jesus and waited a time before he continued to speak.

"I bring you Jesus. As with Herod Antipas, I do not find a reason for judgment against this man. But as it is our custom to release someone at this time from imprisonment, I ask, who do I release? We have the accused thief, Lael, and we have Barabbas who started an insurrection and killed a guard.

And we have Jesus in whom I find no fault. Who do you wish that I release?"

Immediately the cry went up, "Barabbas, we want Barabbas." The crowd was frenzied with chants for release of Barabbas.

Evidently, this surprised Pilate as he stepped back and spoke with someone also on the platform with him.

Pilate moved forward again and spoke directly to the almost-out-of-control crowd that shouted for the release of a murderer. "What do I do with this Jesus then?"

"Crucify Him, crucify Him, crucify Him..." These few words were chanted over and over, louder and louder.

Pilate moved as close to the railing on the platform as possible, pointed at Jesus and shouted, "What crime has this man done? He is not worthy of death."

But the rowdy crowd could not be subdued. Pilate must have known that the crowd would be entirely out of control in a short time.

Amariah and I stood in disbelief from all of the hostility around us. How many of these people had been affected by Jesus or had a family member or acquaintance healed or restored in some manner by Jesus? And now this? I did not know how to react. As with Amariah, all I did was openly cry.

Pilate made several sweeping motions and talked with the guards. We watched as a table with a hand washing vessel was brought out. I wondered at Pilate's theatrics. The crowd was also interested as they became a bit more civil.

"I wash my hands of the responsibility of this matter. You have chosen to crucify an innocent man. His blood is upon you. I do not find him guilty," said Pilate.

But the frenetic crowd returned the unbelievable responses of: "Crucify Him! His blood be upon us! Crucify Jesus!"

The Roman soldiers then took Jesus and returned back into the doorway from which they had brought Him out.

"Amariah, now what? I cannot believe this is happening!" I cried.

Amariah was too emotional to respond. So, we waited. As did this, for the most part, ugly crowd. Many continued cursing and yelling for crucifixion.

"Oh, God," I heard Amariah pray loudly, "please provide a miracle now!"

Someone on the left of Amariah heard this short prayer and slapped Amariah across the face.

We were unsafe here as believers in Jesus; but what is that to what Jesus has suffered, I thought.

And so, we waited; we were weary with the wait and the unknown. This we both knew: Roman punishment was immediate and cruel. Their favored corporal punishment was crucifixion. I knew that from having seen men along the roads leading into and out of Jerusalem. The men were hung by their wrists and feet to a crossed beamed tree until life drained from them. These images swirled in my mind. I felt almost faint.

From another door opening in the area of the governor's fortress, a Roman guard moved out. Armed with swords and shields, a number of soldiers ran into a four-man formation. The soldiers made the crowd move back; the crowd's angry shouts abated.

Two men, who also looked badly beaten, were brought out; they were placed between rows of the soldiers and each had the bulky, cross-beamed death devices placed on their obviously-wounded, naked backs.

Yoshi of Bethlehem

Jesus was then brought out. I could not fully see Him at first. I could only see more soldiers run out. Then the guard moved forward, and I saw Jesus and the third cross-beamed death device that I had hoped not to see. This cruel punishment was meant for Jesus too. But Jesus was not carrying this crossed-beam, another man had this on his back.

The crowd opened as the Romans moved forward with the beaten men and with Jesus. Amariah and I stood stiff and with our arms locked, as this entourage moved past where we were in the crowd. As He neared, I saw a horrific sight. My Messiah had been further beaten, there was no doubt. He had blood flowing from fresh wounds. It appeared that an attempt had been made to clean up His wounds, but crusty looking blood mingled with the fresh was seen at his mouth, in his beard, and at his hairline. His robe clung to His back in swaths of red blood. It was apparent there had been much more abuse suffered by my Lord since he was first brought out by Pilate.

I silently prayed as Amariah and I then followed the soldiers and Jesus through the streets of Jerusalem. I knew Jesus was God and that He could have summoned celestial beings or could have changed the course of the wind or could do whatever He wanted to make the current situation go away.

"What would He do?" I thought.

We walked up a long hill with the crowd. People were now more subdued than when before Pilate. Amariah informed me that this area was called "Golgotha" which means "place of the skull." An ugly name for an ugly place of torture. Maybe the crowd finally realized the significance of this crucifixion. Their loud, unrestrained angry screams were now replaced by more muffled ones. Or perhaps I was hearing only my own muffled screams as they washed over me.

Amariah and I could not get very close to Jesus, but we knew from the crowd's now subdued chatter, and the sickening sound of the thuds of large mallets that struck metal on wood, that He was being crucified. A group in front of us closest to the actual crucifixion site finally began to kneel. That provided Amariah and me with a glimpse of the horrific scene: Jesus was suspended between the two other men. Jesus' face was contorted from the pain. His eyes were closed.

With the crowd quiet, we heard bantering from the guards and the Jewish leaders in front of the crucifixion site. They mocked Jesus and told Him to save Himself if He truly was God. The two others being crucified were thieves, we found out later. But they, too, cursed Jesus and made fun of His claim that He was God.

The Romans hurled a large insult above Him in that they posted a sign which read, "This is Jesus, King of the Jews."

Soldiers walked around Him; they laughed, pointed, and taunted.

Women appeared before Him who wailed loudly, not only from the Jewish custom but from personal grief, I suspected. Jesus spoke to them. I wondered who they might be.

But the smug attitudes and the mockery of Jesus did not last long. Darkness descended and settled down upon the land. It was daytime, but it appeared to be night. With this darkness came increased crying and wailing from people in the crowd. Many must have known this darkness was Providential and felt repentant for their ill-will towards Jesus.

I stood with Amariah in the dark and wondered if some catastrophic event would kill us all. Maybe that was His final plan. I was bereft of all feeling except helplessness.

After quite some time, Jesus cried out. With those words, His body slumped on the cross-beamed wood. My Messiah was crucified.

Jesus died.

Just as Jesus shouted, the earth shook forcefully enough to knock all who stood to the ground. Rocks around us dislodged and rained down on the crowd. I actually sustained a large slice on my ankle from a rock being hurled from the hill before us.

The frenzied crowd who had asked for Jesus' crucifixion was now in another frenzy; they walked back and forth, cried, and audibly begged for forgiveness. Many loudly wailed, "Surely this man was God." Others cried, "What have we done today?"

But He would not answer this day. God's voice was silenced. What did this mean for me, for my family, for others, for redemption of sin?

Amariah and I sat down for some time and neither of us spoke. The darkness slowly lifted.

Finally, Amariah leaned in and told me that Jesus had taught them that if He was "high and lifted up, He would draw all men to Him." Amariah said the Light had come; this was

Yoshi of Bethlehem

His plan. Men were already drawing closer as they repented of their evil in wanting Him crucified. In fact, in the new Light dawning on mid-day, Roman guards knelt before Jesus; perhaps they, too, realized the importance of this One who hung before them.

Amariah knew in his heart and shared with me that the King would have the last word. God's voice was not forever silenced. He would never be silenced!

The darkness continued to lift. I wondered how much of Jerusalem, even Israel, had been covered by this unusual darkness. But it was a dark day for me. My Messiah had been crucified. I was spiritually confused.

Through the now semi-darkness a man approached and walked directly to Amariah.

"Yoshi, it is James…" Amariah explained. "James, my brother, God be praised…" Amariah made a quick introduction of me to James.

"Amariah!" James exclaimed, as he fell on Amariah's neck and wept. "Where do we go now? What do we do? To whom do we turn? He was our life!"

"Yes," said Amariah. "You are almost right. He was our Life. But He is still our Life. Life forever. Life eternal. You know that He taught us that He would not create a kingdom here as many had hoped. You know, James, Jesus told us that He would go to prepare a place for us. His natural body has died. But Life will triumph. Be patient and wait for Him. This is not the end. Think of all the prophecies of old still yet to unfold."

"Amariah, you are the learned and faithful one among us!" James responded.

"Amariah, Yoshi, please come with me. Peter, James, John, the other disciples, they are close to the cross. They wanted to know you are here, Amariah."

I followed Amariah and James who had not released his arm from around Amariah's neck. I am amazed that Amariah knew James so well and that Amariah knew these other disciples of Jesus that James had named. I knew Amariah had been expelled from The School of Law, but only now I realized that my brother had spent all of his time after that expulsion with Jesus and His followers. That is how Amariah knew Jesus' teachings that he so freely shared with me.

It was not an easy task to get to Jesus. I found in life that it never is. But I knew it would be worth the effort. There were many in the way; some were reverent believers while others yet gawked and laughed at the lifeless, earthly body of The Messiah. I did not believe as I started this day with its uncertainties that He would die, but I began to understand that a greater purpose would be served through His death.

As we approached the area of the crosses, Jesus' body was lifted from the upright cross beam onto the ground. I saw several women there with cloths intended for burial; they were the women who had been wailing. I wished we were closer to see all that happened to The Messiah.

Peter, James, John, others (whose names I learned later) greeted Amariah; it was no unfamiliar greeting. It was quite apparent that these were close acquaintances of my brother. The men were both joyful and sad. They wept on one another, yet somehow they turned that weeping into rejoicing; I wished I could hear this latter sentiment, but I stood too far from them. It is still hard to explain how these men reacted to the One whom they loved as He was crucified, but they certainly were not downcast.

James released his hold on Amariah and took up residence beside me. I was thankful for that, since I was not sure what was happening and who was who among this group. James informed me that Jesus' body was taken for burial. A large crowd again followed. I followed out of necessity, as the crowd pushed and shoved in their attempt to remain close to Jesus. Staying close to Jesus, even in death, seemed the correct thing to do. Amariah was ahead but turned to look for me; he seemed relieved when he eyed James still with me. It was apparent Amariah was "at home" with these men who had been with Jesus.

Chapter 20: Finished

Amariah, James, and I and the entourage of disciples and other followers of Jesus walked to a mountain area where tombs were hewn in the sides of the hills. One of these was provided for Jesus' tomb, I later understood from Amariah. James and I were too far away to know what happened at Jesus' tomb. All we knew was that the crowd had stopped, and we could not advance.

It was late in the afternoon, and James remained a constant companion with me. Amariah had left us; he flitted about like a bee moving from flower to flower as he talked with men who James pointed out were all disciples of Jesus. He talked, too, with women who had been faithful supporters and believers in Jesus as well. Jesus' own mother, Mary, was present, I was told.

Amariah made his way back to me and James from the tomb area. Amariah was saddened by the events of the day, but he was also excited, as he told James and me. It was a great emotional contradiction.

"They have placed His body in the tomb. I am not sure if death can hold Our Messiah. We will wait to know," said Amariah with no real despondency in his voice. He continued, "Yoshi, I would like to go back by the Temple. Do you wish to go or should I walk you home to Uncle Roshan's? I know it has already been a long and emotionally charged day."

"Brother, I am going with you," I said with no hesitation.

James and the other disciples remained at the tomb. It had not been sealed, and the disciples made sure all was done according to Jewish Law and with no chicanery from the Romans. Sabbath approached; all had to be done quickly.

Amariah and I made our regress into Jerusalem and to the Temple area. It was no small feat considering the masses surrounding us. Due to the crucifixion and because it was Passover, the streets were thronged with people and rams and lambs and doves in cages and on poles and pack animals and carts. Again, we were forced to walk without talking; it was just too crowded and too loud for any conversation.

Yoshi of Bethlehem

This gave me time to reflect on this day to this point. My thoughts raced, like my beloved flock when frightened. I was overwhelmed by spiritual and natural emotion, but this feeling was more awe-inspiring than crushing. My Messiah was crucified, yet Amariah and the other disciples were not unsettled by this action. The short time I heard them speak was a repeat of Amariah's words to James that Jesus talked about being lifted high on the third day. Of what consequence was this comment?

As we neared the grand Temple edifice, it was apparent that the crowd here had experienced a significant encounter during the day. Many sat quietly in prayer; others stood gazing up. All seemed as reverent as usual at the Temple. Perhaps they just learned the news of Jesus' death. I was not certain. It appeared no organized lines waited for entrance to make sacrifice; however, there was a great throng of people going into and out of the central area and into the Court of the Gentiles. They made their entrance and exit from the area in too much haste and without a beast for sacrifice. What could this mean?

"Yoshi," said Amariah, "follow me closely." And with that, we entered into an area where typically only Temple workers go. It was not a high holy area; it was used for animal and instrument cleansing. We passed through this area to the Court of the Gentiles without dealing with the multitude already present.

We then took a swift turn and entered a low building which had scant light. I had to mind where Amariah walked while I avoided sacrificial meat pieces and bowls laid out in vast quantities on low slung tables with hooks. It could have really been an interesting place to visit under other circumstances.

Finally, Amariah led us out into the daylight and up some stairs. We could see the Temple proper from the vantage point of this building's portico.

"Yoshi," exclaimed Amariah, obviously not caring if he was seen or heard, "look. Into the Temple, look!"

I looked where he pointed.

"I do not know what I am seeing, Amariah."

"There is openness inside. The curtain, the veil of the Temple. It is separated. That must be what the people keep passing by to try to see. It used to hang so you could not see inside the Temple toward the Holy of Holies. That veil was thick, and you could not see behind it, above it, beneath it. I had hoped to one day be a High Priest who could pass that veil to enter the holiest place where God's Presence dwelt. It is apparent that now Jesus has opened that opportunity to all. The veil has been parted. This is an awesome happening!"

"Amariah," called a voice to our left. "What are you doing here?" queried that voice as its owner came into view. It was an older priest in his official attire.

"Caleb Ben-Ashur, I have come from the crucifixion site of Jesus to understand what that might have meant to the Temple," explained Amariah. "This is my brother, Yoshi."

This priest obviously meant no harm to Amariah, although he surely realized that we should not be where we were, especially considering Amariah had been dismissed from the Priesthood.

"Today was a day of reckoning for Israel, I believe, Amariah. There was darkness upon the earth for some time; we had been sacrificing when the darkness descended. Passover is such a holy time, and there are many sacrifices to be made, as you know, Amariah. We Priests were all frightened by this darkness, this celestial occurrence, and were in awe of its meaning. We had been informed that the man, Jesus, was being executed by the Romans. I knew, Amariah, that the darkness was of God for our sin of unbelief toward Jesus. I personally asked forgiveness during this time for my unbelief of Him. I am now willing to consider that this was no ordinary man, no ordinary teacher. Perhaps…perhaps, this Jesus was Messiah."

Caleb continued, "I was in deep contemplation within the Temple. I did not want to be out in the darkness itself. But suddenly I heard what I can only call a loud clap, like thunder maybe, and then the veil of the Temple was torn from the top to the bottom. How could something so thick just sever into two pieces? We Priests began to wail and lament. For me, it was a time of reflection of my disbelief and disregard of the One called Jesus. We asked among ourselves about the meaning of the veil being torn. No one could fathom its importance. But you are here, Amariah. What significance does this have? Please tell me. I know you have been with Jesus on many occasions and have seen many marvelous things and have heard the Master teach. What could this mean?"

"Caleb, I believe that this is a sign from God that the Priesthood as we have known it is over. The Messiah came to save people, not from Roman rule to make Israel a great kingdom as so many hoped and believed, but Jesus came to save people from their sins. No more would this require a blood sacrifice, Caleb and Yoshi. Jesus became The Sacrifice to atone for all of mankind. His blood was shed to cover all our sins. As David told us would happen, 'He was poured out like water.' I believe the veil was torn to reveal we are all now able to go to God personally; the curtain does not keep us away from His Presence, from His Holiness."

Caleb became weak-kneed at this thought and slid into a sitting position on the porch. His face grew ashen, and he stared into the crowd blankly.

"Caleb, you must decide how you wish to continue your spiritual journey. Even if you remain a priest, you can no longer deny Jesus Christ."

With that statement made by Amariah, this priest fell backward from his sitting position, as if in death. But he was breathing, that I could see.

Amariah stooped and spoke to him in his ear very quietly for a short time. The priest did not stir.

Amariah rose and turned to me. His face reflected something I cannot explain. His speaking to the older priest brought a calm and sweet Presence into that area. Was this how we were to continue, to speak about Jesus to anyone who would listen?

"Yoshi," Amariah began, "we can continue home. Caleb is in a state of spiritual meditation. He may be that way for some time. I think we have found from Caleb what we wanted to know of the day's occurrences here at Temple. We should return home. It will be dark soon. We should rest. We may need to go and find the disciples later."

And with that, Amariah moved us through the low building with all the animal parts and the priestly vessels once again and out of the Court of the Gentiles, past The Court of the Women, through the Temple area and into the street.

We entered the street just as several mounted Roman soldiers rode past. One of those soldiers broke rank—it was Marcus.

He dismounted, ran to us, and threw his arms around both our necks and began to cry and shout.

"I was there; I was there. I saw it. No, I saw Him. I saw Jesus as my God. I saw the crucifixion. I know now that I have been lost. The love that came from Jesus while all around Him others reviled Him and ridiculed Him was astounding. I can no longer remain silent. I now believe in Jesus. The darkness, the land groaning as it did, it was all for my benefit. He died for me to know that He was Messiah..." Marcus' voice trailed off.

Amariah praised God aloud. "Jesus, be praised. Jesus, you are great and victorious..."

The crowd moved closer to hear all that was shouted by both Marcus and Amariah. I instinctively knew this was no time for me to remain silent either. I, too, shouted aloud praises to Jesus; I had never voiced my adoration of The Messiah. It was exhilarating!

The crowd leapt around us and praised as well. It was as if God were present right there; a feeling I could describe only as ecstasy erupted around us. The three of us began to dance; the Shekinah Glory of God (as Amariah explained it to me later; this spirit had come on priests in the past) fell on us. Was this the way it would be going forward? I did not know how long we were at the Temple gates as we praised and worshiped Jesus. I knew only that it was dark and the crowd around us had dispersed when the three of us then set out to find Lydia and take her with us to Uncle Roshan's. We wanted everyone together as we gave discourse of the events of the day, a day I will never forget.

Sharon Mullen

Uncle Roshan and Cousin Ketab were present when we all arrived back to his house well after sundown. Uncle Roshan was somewhat taken aback at our exuberance over Jesus' crucifixion. He could not understand that this was only the beginning of the spiritual future for Israel—and all of mankind. We did not grieve his crucifixion; we looked forward to what Jesus had planned. Lydia, as well as the rest of the family there, was captivated at Marcus' confession that he now believed in Jesus as God. We all praised Jesus for Marcus' transformation at the cross. Golgotha, that place of great loss was also a place of great gain for Marcus, other Roman guards, and many Jews who were present that day. Indeed it was a place of great gain for all the world!

As I write this chapter of my story, I cannot fail to speak of the happenings after Jesus' death. Amariah's insight into prophecies of old due to his being taught by the greatest Teacher of all was invaluable.

Jesus was entombed as witnessed by His disciples and his mother and several other women who had ministered to Jesus and His disciple. These women had helped the disciples in their time of hunger and sickness and need while Jesus was alive. Roman guards were actually stationed by the tomb

Yoshi of Bethlehem

because Pilate was told about Jesus' claim that He would rise in three days. The Romans felt perhaps the disciples would take His body and make a spurious claim that He did rise. Despite the Romans' best attempts at keeping Jesus in that guarded tomb, however, He did arise on the third day as He had previously taught that He would.

Mary the Mother of Jesus and Mary Magdalene and other women went to Jesus' tomb to anoint his body with spices and found it empty and the Roman guards not standing guard! The ladies ran back into town and alerted the disciples. Peter and John journeyed there quickly and saw the tomb as the women said they would: empty!

But Jesus Himself appeared to the disciples, including my brother, Amariah, and other devout followers of Jesus while they were gathered after the crucifixion. Jesus told them to continue in prayer and that they were to receive great power after the "Holy Spirit" was come upon them. What this Holy Spirit was, no one knew. Jesus showed Himself to the disciples on various occasions and taught them more. Forty days after He rose from the dead, Jesus led them to Bethany. There, Jesus ascended into the heavens. They watched Him as He was supernaturally transported into the clouds, and they could no longer see Him.

But this was not a day of sadness that He was physically gone. They were excited at the prospect of this promised Holy Spirit and power. They believed and prayed for this happening. And the disciples were aware of a sense of His Presence every time they spoke His Name in worship or prayed for a specific need.

Though unsure about this Holy Spirit, they waited together for some days in prayer and meditation and fasting. The disciples wanted whatever Jesus promised them, and they did what Jesus had instructed them, "tarry in Jerusalem until they were filled with power!" The Feast of Pentecost came, ten days after Jesus had ascended into heaven, and there were one-hundred and twenty followers of Christ in a room where they had prayed every day since Jesus' ascension.

On feast day, they prayed to Jesus as they often did, but something spectacular, something supernatural occurred. I can write about this now as Amariah was there; Amariah participated; Amariah was changed to being even more zealous about Jesus afterwards.

Yoshi of Bethlehem

As they prayed, a noise was heard, and a strong breeze blew upon all who were there. And then, as Amariah explained it, everyone in that room began to praise God in many diverse languages; those who praised Him were not speaking in their native tongues. How long they rejoiced and praised Jesus in the other languages, Amariah was not sure. It was a long time, and no one felt to leave. Amariah said it was the same Spirit he had felt when Marcus had met us after the crucifixion, and we had worshiped. But the speaking in another language seemed to move each one to another level with spiritual power. Jesus had told them when He left in Bethany to wait for this power. Amariah was exuberant in his claim that it was well worth the wait!

So this was the Spirit that Jesus had promised; all left that room having felt a higher power and a deeper call to work for Jesus the Christ. Some, like Peter, John, and Matthew were used to doing miracles among the sick and mentally and spiritually disturbed, just as Jesus had done. Others returned to their home cities as they rejoiced and shared the news of what had occurred.

There were, of course, others who returned to their previous lives within the community of the Jewish spiritual leaders. They had witnessed many miracles; they had felt the power that had been promised by the Spirit that fell each time they gathered; they rejoiced for a short time in the revelation that Jesus was Messiah. But they could not reconcile their traditional teachings with the new teachings that Jesus wanted to be put forth through the disciples.

Amariah quoted Jesus when he spoke of some of these men who returned to their old ways. Jesus had told them many would not believe even though they saw great signs and wonders. Messiah had told a crowd one day that "the way that leads to life was straight and narrow and that few would choose to enter there. Instead, they preferred the wide path, the easy way that actually would lead to their spiritual destruction."

It was during the time that the disciples waited together in Jerusalem that Amariah received great honor from the disciples. This man, my brother, who had been taught in Scripture but had been rejected by the Jewish leaders was, as Amariah told me later, "greatly humbled by his exalted standing within the disciples of Jesus." For my brother, whose real name is Mattityahu Amariah, was elected to be numbered among the Twelve Disciples. His name as a disciple was used in the Greek: Matthias.

Amariah, or Matthias, continued to preach and teach about Jesus Christ until his last breath.

There are so many miraculous events relating to Jesus to chronicle. I do not have enough time with the scribe here now to tell of all.

I do wish to mention that Philip and Amariah remained steadfast friends for life. Phillip taught about Jesus as Messiah for many years; he died on a journey to teach others.

Philip's brother, Saul, is certainly very worth mentioning. His hatred of Jesus and His followers was not hidden; he was undoubtedly behind Pilate's decision to crucify the Lord. Saul had even more work to accomplish after the power of God fell at the Feast of Pentecost; as the disciples and other followers of Christ shamelessly and fearlessly taught and preached of Jesus, more and more Jews, and then Gentiles, believed in Him. As Jesus had told Nicodemus when He taught about a new birth, people were being baptized in water and of the Spirit. Saul actually had clearance from the Chief Priests to arrest any believers. As men returned home to many cities beyond Jerusalem after the feast and shared with

others about Jesus, many came to believe in Him! Mock trials
Saul set up saw that believers were imprisoned for heresy and
other infractions of Jewish Law. Many feared Saul and his
cadre of jackals who pounced on followers of Christ.

However, Saul was miraculously transformed by a personal revelation that Jesus was Messiah. Saul then realized
he had indeed done wrong to harass, imprison, and even kill
those who taught about Jesus. This change in his life meant
a total eschewing of all old spiritual thinking and made Saul
an unabashed religious zealot! His conversion led many to
Christ. I am sure I can never know the full extent of this man's
life. He even assumed his Latin name of Paul, perhaps to reflect the significant changes in his life!

My scribe has another appointment, and thus I must
make the rest of my thoughts concise.

I, Yoshi of Bethlehem, felt compelled to write these words
because of the great blessing my family and I have enjoyed as
a result of Jesus the Christ. The joys experienced because
we believe in Jesus are innumerable. I began as a shepherd
when a young lad and continued that vocation throughout
my life and have passed down this noble work to my sons.
My hero, David, was a shepherd, and that is of great con-

sequence to me. But to have known of, and to have experienced, the Great Shepherd is unfathomable. It is also hard
to adequately describe. Jesus became the embodiment and
spirit of the Psalm of David I loved best: "The Lord is my
Shepherd; I shall not want."